Just Lucky

THE OUTSIDERS
THE SONNETS

Just Lucky

Melanie Florence

Second Story Press

Library and Archives Canada Cataloguing in Publication

Title: Just Lucky / Melanie Florence.
Names: Florence, Melanie, author.
Identifiers: Canadiana (print) 20190074949 | Canadiana (ebook) 20190074957 | ISBN 9781772601046 (softcover) | ISBN 9781772601053 (EPUB)
Classification: LCC PS8611.L668 J88 2019 | DDC jC813/.6—dc23

Cover and illustrations by Katy Dockrill
Edited by Kathryn White
Design by Melissa Kaita

Printed and bound in Canada

Second Story Press gratefully acknowledges the support of the Ontario Arts Council and the Canada Council for the Arts for our publishing program. We acknowledge the financial support of the Government of Canada through the Canada Book Fund.

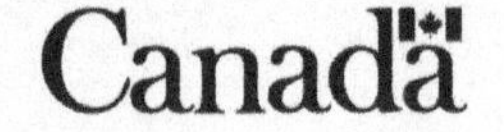

Published by
Second Story Press
20 Maud Street, Suite 401
Toronto, ON M5V 2M5
www.secondstorypress.ca

MIX
Paper from responsible sources
FSC® C004071

For my grandmother, Anne, on whom Lucky's grandma is based.

For my grandfather, Alfred, who reminds me of Lucky's grandpa.

And for Taylor, who is a badass like Lucky.

CHAPTER ONE
Just the Three of Us

My mother named me Lucky. I swear. It's on my birth certificate and everything.

My grandma used to tell me that my mom would go to the casino when she was pregnant and rub her belly for luck. Apparently she won a jackpot and decided then and there that I was her good-luck charm. At least until I was born and she discovered she couldn't bring a newborn to the casino for hours at a time. Or forget about her entirely and leave her beside a slot machine while she smoked crack in the parking lot.

"That fool girl," as Grandma called her, got herself arrested, and I was left with grandparents who were long done with their own parenting but took over the care and feeding of another kid without a second thought.

So for the past fifteen years, it has just been the three of us: Grandma, Grandpa, and me. Lucky Robinson. I've only seen my mother a handful of times since she gave me up. She calls every couple of years or so when she's desperate for money, but it's been ages since I saw her last. I'm not even sure I could pick her out of a police lineup at this point. To be honest, I secretly believe that I'll be asked to do that someday.

I watched the cursor flashing on the screen and then deleted everything I had just written. I was pretty sure Mr. Alexander hadn't had this in mind when he asked us to write a My Story essay for language arts. Maybe I should just make up something a little more PG-rated and get an easy A. Something like: I was born into a happy family with 2.5 kids, a white picket fence, and a golden retriever named Billy the Kid. Or Henry. Or Finn. I don't know. I've always been bad at naming pets. I once had a stuffed bird named Princess Featherfingers. Don't ask me why. I had a stuffed dog named Mr. Ages Sparklehead too. I was really big on formal titles for my animals apparently.

God, I hate the look of a blank screen. That flashing cursor was definitely judging my lack of a normal family to write about.

"Lucky?"

"In here, Grandma." I could hear the soft hush of her slippers shuffling toward me before I saw her.

"Why are you studying in the dining room?" she asked, pulling gently on my ponytail, something she had been doing since I was a kid.

"Because if I study in my room, I'll fall asleep."

"Fair enough. Can you get your grandfather and tell him dinner will be ready soon?"

"He's not here."

"He's not...where is he?"

"He's helping Mr. Tate move a couch or a chair or something. Actually, I think it's a bed. I don't know. I was only half listening when he told you."

"He didn't tell me he was going out." She frowned.

"Yes, he did," I said carefully. "Remember, Grandma? He told you he had to help move...something. And you said he'd better be back for dinner or you'd eat his dessert."

"Lemon merengue pie," she finished. "His favorite."

"Right!"

"Hmph. All right then. Could you set the table, please?"

"Sure. I can finish this later." I closed my laptop, ready to leave that judgy blank screen behind for a while. "Grandma?"

"Mmhm?" She was gathering up my notebooks in a pile and wiping the table under them.

"Are you okay?"

She snapped her dish towel at me in response.

"Hurry up. Your grandfather will be back from the store any minute."

"He's not...yeah, okay..." I trailed off, staring at her back as she headed toward the kitchen, humming something under her breath that sounded oddly like the theme song from *Doctor Who*.

CHAPTER TWO
Old Not Stupid

Grandma was still puttering around the kitchen when my grandfather wandered into the house.

"Dinner ready?" he asked, hanging his flannel jacket up in the hall closet. "I could eat a horse."

"I never understood what that meant," I mused. "Why would anyone want to eat a horse?"

"Smartass." He leaned down and gave me a kiss on the head. He smelled like aftershave and outdoors. And a faint, lingering hint of pipe tobacco.

"If Grandma catches you smoking, you can forget about dinner," I told him.

"Cover for me. I'll go jump in the shower."

"She thinks you went to the store," I told him. "Her memory is getting worse, isn't it?" He studied me for a long moment and then smiled gently.

"She's all right, Lucky. She's just getting old."

"Are you sure that's all it is? Because she left the water running in the shower again this morning. It was like a rain forest in there."

"You don't have to worry. Grandma is fine. She's just forgetful, I promise. It happens when you get old. You forget things. Like I forgot she doesn't like me smoking and had a nice pipe and a coffee with Mr. Tate." He winked.

"Oh, that's hilarious. I'm sure she'll love that one. Why don't we call her in here right now and tell her?" I teased. This was our routine. I'd worry and he'd diffuse it with a joke. It usually worked.

"Don't you dare! Just hold her off for five minutes while I shower."

He tousled my hair and dashed from the room. Even at his age—which I was constantly reminding him was too advanced to be up on ladders or carrying furniture—he still moved at a pace faster than most teenagers.

I tried to ignore it like I always did, but something about Grandma was off, and I couldn't help but wonder if maybe she needed to see her doctor. I had said as much to him before, but he always brushed me off. Grandma had been afraid of doctors since she was a kid, and no matter how you prepared her or promised it was just an exam, she was convinced one was going to randomly pop out and jab her with a needle or something.

"Did I hear your grandfather?" Grandma poked her head back into the living room, disheveled from the heat of the stove she had been standing over.

"Yeah. He'll be down in a second. He just wanted a quick shower."

She smiled. "Smoking that damned pipe again?"

"You know about that?" I asked, flabbergasted.

"I'm old. Not stupid, Lucky. Anyway, he probably needed it after helping Mr. Tate all day. Come grab the pot roast and put it out for me, would you?"

All I could manage was a weak nod. Sometimes I worried about her until I made myself sick. Then she'd be her usual self again like nothing had happened. My friend Alex said her grandparents were the same, so maybe Grandpa was right, and I was worrying for no reason. Then I thought about the shower that had run for so long that the bathroom was engulfed in a haze so thick I couldn't see my hand in front of my face.

"Lucky!"

"Right! Coming." I'd think about it later, I decided, heading into the kitchen to grab the pot roast.

CHAPTER THREE
Comfort

After dinner, Grandma retired to the living room with her remote and a cup of tea.

"*Jeopardy* time!" she said happily to no one in particular.

Grandma loved her game shows.

Grandpa was elbows-deep in suds, sponging a glass before putting it on the draining board.

"You know she'll make you do them all over again if you don't rinse," I reminded him.

"Not if you don't tell her," Grandpa flicked some bubbles at me. "Grab a towel."

I did, rinsing the dishes with exaggerated movements.

"You're awful!" Grandpa laughed. "Hurry up though."

"Why? Did you want to catch the thrilling second half of *Jeopardy?*" I asked, gesturing toward the living room where we could hear Grandma shouting at the TV.

"*The Great Gatsby!*" she yelled out.

"For someone who can't remember to turn the shower off, she has a pretty amazing memory for literature." I giggled.

"And world history," Grandpa interjected.

"And pop culture," I added.

"And completely random facts that no other human alive knows." Grandpa smiled.

"Yes! How *does* she know all those weird little facts?"

"Your grandmother is a genius who reads everything she can get her hands on."

"She does love to read," I grinned back.

"That reminds me!" he said, drying his hands on a tea towel.

"Of what?"

"I got you something." He dashed to the front door and came back holding a paper bag.

"What's that?" I asked, putting the last plate in the cupboard and hanging the dish towel on the towel rack.

"Come sit down," Grandpa called, patting the chair beside him. He dumped the contents of the bag onto the table.

"Oh my god!" I squealed, picking the first book up, then another. *Gone With the Wind! The Three Musketeers, The Hobbit, The Sonnets of William Shakespeare!* I looked at Grandpa, who was grinning widely at me. "Grandpa! Where did you get these?"

"I stopped at the used bookstore. They had a deal: fill a bag for a buck."

"You got all these books for a dollar?" I shuffled through

the rest of the pile. "*The Outsiders, A Wrinkle in Time, Sherlock Holmes?* Grandpa, this is amazing! Thank you!" I abandoned the pile of books to throw my arms around him.

"You're welcome, Lucky." He hugged me back fiercely like he always did, and I wondered for the millionth time what I'd done to deserve him and my grandmother. Just Lucky, I guess. "What are you going to read first?" he asked.

I looked down at the table at the wealth of new reading material he had found for me.

"Wow. Umm...I'm not sure. How about...*The Hobbit?*" I held it up for him to see.

"Yes! Excellent choice. I'll grab us some snacks, you find a good reading spot for us."

"Grandpa, listen to this...isn't it the best opening of a book ever?

"In a hole in the ground there lived a hobbit. Not a nasty, dirty, wet hole, filled with the ends of worms and an oozy smell, nor yet a dry, bare, sandy hole with nothing in it to sit down on or to eat: it was a hobbit-hole, and that means comfort."

CHAPTER FOUR
The Boy Next Door

The blast of a car horn signaled my ride to school had arrived.

"Lucky! Ryan's here!" Grandma called out.

"I heard," I grumbled, grabbing my lunch. I was in no way, shape, or form a morning person.

"Give him this." She stuck a piece of bannock smothered in maple butter wrapped in a paper towel into my hands. It was still warm and smelled absolutely heavenly.

"Don't I get any?" I asked.

She handed me another piece and kissed my cheek.

"Have a good day, sweetie."

"Thanks, Grandma. You too," I called over my shoulder.

"Whatcha got for me?" Ryan called before I had even made it to his car. His eyes were gray today. Stormy. He was one of those people whose eyes changed from blue to green to gray.

I flopped into the passenger seat and handed him the bannock.

"Awesome!" He had half of it in his mouth before we had even left my driveway.

I laughed. Only Ryan could make me laugh before noon.

Ryan was my first and best friend. We were both seven when he moved next door. He was, quite literally, the boy next door. I was sitting on the front porch, feeling sorry for myself and wishing I had a normal mom like all the other kids, when a little blond boy with his hair sticking up in spikes kicked a soccer ball into the steps at my feet.

"Hey," he said, studying me as he retrieved his ball.

"Hey," I sniffled, wiping my face on my sleeve.

"Want to play?" he asked, nodding at the ball.

I shrugged.

"Come on. I'll teach you."

He smiled widely, showing off two missing front teeth.

I smiled back. I couldn't help it. I still can't.

"Yeah, okay." I climbed down from the porch and kicked the ball back toward him.

By the end of the afternoon, Ryan was sitting at our kitchen table eating chocolate chip cookies still warm from the oven and promising to share his comic books with me. I had a pretty impressive collection myself, thanks to Grandpa, so I promised to do the same.

Grandma placed a glass of ice-cold milk in front of each of us and tried to poke Ryan's hair into submission.

He grinned.

"It just grows that way," he said, stuffing another cookie into his mouth and chasing it with long gulps of milk. By the time he left, we had made plans to explore my basement together the next day and had already decided we were going to be best friends forever.

Fast forward eight years and here we were. Some things hadn't changed. Some had. He had discovered hair products so that crazy sticky-uppy hair of his had been tamed into some kind of submission. But he wasn't the boy next door anymore.

CHAPTER FIVE
Checkmate

"How's your grandma?" Ryan asked, drumming his fingers on the steering wheel along with the music.

"Fine. You know. Same as always," I told him, staring out the window.

"Yeah? That's good. I know she had you worried...forgetting stuff." I could feel him glancing over at me.

"Oh, that. She's doing better."

"Really? Did she see a doctor?"

"I don't know. I guess. Listen, have you figured out how you're going to ask Thomas to prom?"

"Yes! I saw this guy on YouTube asking his boyfriend out, and it was so awesome!"

Ryan kept babbling on about his crush and pulling off the perfect promposal. I nodded, tuning him out and thinking about my grandma. The truth was, she wasn't any better. And it was hard to watch. She had been the strongest of us for as long as I could remember. When Ryan came out two years ago, she had been the one to stand up to his hyper-religious parents. I looked over at Ryan, smiling happily beside me. I had seen him fall out of trees, crash his bike spectacularly, and had stayed up with him an entire night when we were about eighty percent sure he had a concussion. But I never saw him cry until the night he came out to his parents.

It was late. I was finishing up a game of chess with my grandfather using the pieces he had spent countless hours whittling when he was young. I was holding a knight that I had captured, running my fingers over it like a worry stone. It was worn smooth by years of use and had a patina from being held by so many hands. I loved those pieces. I made up stories with them when I was little and then played chess with them when Grandpa taught me. He was staring at the board now.

"Are you ever going to make a move?" I asked him, turning the knight over and over in my fingers.

"Give me a minute," Grandpa said, reaching for one piece and then another.

"I've given you thirty!"

"You're exaggerating." Grandpa laughed, shifting a pawn forward, then back.

"Just move it!" I yelled, giggling.

There was a knock on the door but we ignored it. Grandma was in the kitchen beside the door.

"Don't rush me!" Grandpa said, reaching for his queen.

"Henry!" Grandma called out from the kitchen.

"Just a second, Daisy. I'm about to kick Lucky's butt."

"As if!" I shrieked, throwing a handful of popcorn at him.

"Henry!"

There was something about the tone of Grandma's voice that made Grandpa stop laughing and lunge from his chair. My heart was beating too fast all of a sudden. I followed Grandpa into the kitchen, still clutching the chess piece tightly in my hand.

CHAPTER SIX
Ryan Comes Out

I barely felt the knight fall from my fingers. I didn't see it hit the floor or roll under the table. Ryan was standing in my kitchen where he had stood a million times before.

And he was crying.

Grandma was putting ice in a dish towel and talking in a low voice to Ryan.

He was shaking.

There was blood on his face.

Grandpa grabbed a chair and guided him into it.

"Ryan?" My voice cracked.

I barely recognized it.

I barely recognized *him*.

"What happened?" I asked, falling onto my knees in front of him. "Were you in an accident?"

Ryan's head was in his hands.

"Who did this?" Grandpa asked quietly as Grandma pressed the towel of ice to Ryan's face.

"I...told him...I..." I could barely make out what he was saying.

"Who?" I asked.

"My dad." Ryan looked up.

He looked terrible. His left eye was swollen, and there was a cut on his cheek that was oozing blood. He also looked furious.

"You told him," I breathed. I had never had a father, but I was pretty sure your dad wasn't supposed to beat the shit out of you.

"Told him what?" Grandpa asked.

I looked at Ryan, who nodded slightly.

"That he's gay," I said. Ryan had told me months ago. Truthfully, it had taken me completely by surprise. But once the shock had worn off, I was fine with it. He was still Ryan, after all. Nothing had changed. But his parents weren't like me. Or you. Or anyone normal you've ever met. His parents were religious. But not like, go to church, say grace, love your neighbors religious. Ryan's parents were more the speaking in tongues, condemn you to hell, snake-handling type of Christian.

And I had heard them say more than once that "the gays" could be rehabilitated.

I had told Ryan not to tell them, but he wanted to come out at school, and he figured he should come out to them first. *Big mistake,* I thought, looking at his rapidly swelling face. *Obviously.*

"Your father did this?" Grandma asked. Her expression was thunderous. Oh boy. A storm was definitely brewing in the kitchen.

Ryan nodded.

"Because you told him you're gay?"

Another nod.

"Hold this," she handed the ice pack to Ryan. "I'm going to have a word with your parents."

"Grandma..."

"Don't 'Grandma' me!" Her eyes were blazing. "This..." She gestured at Ryan's bruised face. "*This* is not all right. And it's certainly not 'Christian.'"

"It's okay, Mrs. Robinson," Ryan told her.

"No, son. It most certainly is not." She slammed the door behind her as she stormed out to confront Ryan's parents.

My grandfather looked thoughtful.

"Nikâwiy—my mother—was a Christian woman," he said. "She had two sons. Me and my brother, George. She taught us that Creator loved us." He reached out and shifted the ice that Ryan was holding so that it better covered the swollen spot under his eye. He nodded. "George had a secret for a long time. I thought it was a girlfriend, but when I'd tease him or ask who it was, he'd get upset. I thought it must be some girl from school—someone off the rez. But it wasn't. And his secret was killing him. He didn't eat. Didn't sleep. Nikâwiy finally sat him down one night and told him that he could trust her. She would love him no matter what was going on. I listened from the stairs where no one could see me, and I heard my brother crying, admitting that the person he loved was another boy."

I was staring at my grandfather. I didn't know my Uncle George—he had died before I was born—but I know I had seen photos of him with his partner. But I had never heard my grandfather talk about him like this. Ryan was studying him through his one good eye.

"Nikâwiy told him that Creator doesn't make mistakes. He was exactly as he was supposed to be, and anyone who thought any differently could deal with her." He glanced at me. "Your grandmother reminds me of her in that way." He looked back at Ryan and smiled kindly. "There's nothing wrong with you, son. No matter what your parents say. You're exactly who you're supposed to be. And if you're lucky enough to fall in love, don't you worry about what anyone else thinks. Love is a gift." He took Ryan's hand in his work-worn one and squeezed it gently.

Tears spilled down Ryan's face as he nodded at Grandpa.

Grandma walked back in then, her face no less thunderous than when she had walked out.

"How did it go?" I asked, dreading the answer.

She tossed a bag down on the floor.

"Ryan, you'll stay with us for a while," she said.

CHAPTER SEVEN

Promposal

That's what I loved about my grandmother. She didn't take shit from anyone. She despised intolerance and scoffed at so-called Christians who twisted the Bible to suit themselves.

"That's not *my* Creator," she'd say. I respected that. I guess I felt the same way.

"Are you coming?" Ryan was already out of the car.

"Sorry! Yeah. I'm coming."

I had been going to school with the same kids for so long that every day was basically just like any other. Ryan was immediately scouting the hall for his crush. I waved to Amy from my drama class and nodded to the kid who sat behind me in math. A group of boys on the basketball team high-fived Ryan and ignored me. So, like every other day.

"I'll see you at lunch?" Ryan asked as I stopped at my

locker. We shared afternoon classes, but I was on my own for drama and gym in the morning.

"For sure." I gave him a hug, like always, and headed to my first class. Drama first thing in the morning was tough when you weren't a morning person, but it was far preferable to starting the day off with gym. Drama was something I had loved since my grandparents had started taking me to see plays when I was a kid. There was something about getting lost in someone else's story for a couple of hours that I couldn't get enough of. Maybe because my own story hadn't been anything much to write about. I craved stories about happy families when I was young. Now I just hungered for a great story and characters I cared about.

We did improv, which normally I think I'm pretty good at. Maybe not so much first thing in the morning. But since the first rule of improv is to always say *yes*, I just kind of went with it when my partner asked me if I was a good dog, and I spent the next twenty minutes on my hands and knees, barking at everyone and grabbing Mr. Rosenwald's sleeve in my teeth. The class roared, which woke me up enough to get me to gym and to actually hit the volleyball over the net a few times.

I showered and dressed quickly. It was pizza day in the cafeteria, and my mouth was watering already just thinking of the gooey, melty cheese and the salty bite of the pepperoni. The hallway was already teeming with kids heading to the caf, but since Ryan's last class before lunch was right down the hall, I knew he'd already be there, saving me a seat. And with any luck, he had grabbed me a slice before the line got too long.

I came to a dead stop in the doorway to the cafeteria, causing a bit of a pileup and getting me elbowed in the back for my negligence. Ryan was, indeed, sitting at our usual table, but he wasn't alone. Thomas was perched on the edge, smiling down at him.

I couldn't help it. I felt a twinge of jealousy. Seeing them together…I don't know how to explain it. I was happy Ryan had met someone. Especially someone as nice as Thomas. But it also made me feel, for the first time in my life, like a third wheel. I knew Ryan would try to include me if he ended up dating Thomas. (And it was looking like that really was going to happen.) But seeing things change right before my eyes hit me harder than I thought it would. I wanted him to be happy. He deserved that more than anyone. But I couldn't help feeling—maybe selfishly—that it meant that everything was going to change. It wouldn't be me and Ryan anymore. And I wasn't sure how I was going to deal with that.

I pasted a smile on my face and moved out of the way, walking toward our table.

"Hey, Lucky!" Ryan was beaming. I felt terrible suddenly even thinking for a second about how his dating Thomas would affect me.

"Hey. Hi, Thomas."

"Hi, Lucky." Thomas smiled. "Sorry. I'm in your way, aren't I?"

"No, you're fine. I'll just sit over here." I pointed to a chair on the other side of the table, not at all close to the spot beside Ryan where I usually sat.

"Oh, no. I'll move. I have to go anyway. The basketball team has a meeting to talk about fundraising."

"Let me know if you need any help," Ryan told him. "I'm great at fundraising."

I literally couldn't think of a single time he had ever raised money for anything. But Thomas was smiling down at him in a way that was making the tips of Ryan's ears turn pink.

"I might take you up on that. I'll see you guys later." He waved, dashing off toward the door and, I assumed, the gym. Ryan stared after him, a pretty adorable grin on his face.

"So? Did you ask him yet?" I asked, pulling one of the slices of pizza he had bought toward me. It was pretty obvious to everyone that Thomas was into Ryan too. They'd been dancing around it for most of the school year. But Ryan—being Ryan—wanted it to be spectacular.

"No! Do you seriously think I'm the kind of person who would ask the man of my dreams out in the middle of the cafeteria?" he shuddered.

"Sorry." I rolled my eyes at him, biting into the lukewarm pizza. It was still pretty good. "I'm really not sure what you're waiting for."

"I haven't worked out the logistics yet."

"The logistics? It's a date, Ryan."

"It's prom, Lucky!" He was outraged. "It's got to be perfect. Absolutely memorable."

"You're not still thinking about getting doves, are you? No one wants to be shit on by doves at their promposal, Ryan."

"No. I'm not having doves. But what about a puppy?"

"Why do you have to have live animals?" I asked.

"Puppies are cute!"

This went on for longer than I'm proud of. It literally continued through both math class *and* English, where we passed notes back and forth. We were still arguing when we got in his car and when we pulled into my driveway.

"Do you want to come in for a while?" I asked him, effectively putting an end to an incredibly odd conversation about the merits of using teacup pigs to ask Thomas out.

"Nah. I promised my aunt I'd help her with dinner."

Probably a good thing. I'd eaten his aunt's cooking.

"All right. Tell Aunt Maggie hi."

"I will. And I'll text you later if I come up with anything for the promposal."

"I'll be waiting breathlessly," I promised.

Much as I teased him, I was hoping it would all go off without a hitch. He deserved that. No one deserved a happily ever after more than Ryan after what he'd been through with his parents.

CHAPTER EIGHT
Grandpa

I let the door slam shut behind me. I knew Grandma hated that, but the usual shout from the kitchen didn't come.

"Grandma?" I called out.

"Shhh!" She bustled down the stairs in front of me. "Your grandfather isn't feeling well. He's lying down."

"What's wrong with him?" I asked. Grandpa was never sick. He always seemed immune to all the colds that Grandma and I usually passed back and forth.

"I don't know," she fussed. "He's poorly." She pushed past me and started banging around in the kitchen. Probably making soup. She always made soup no matter what the ailment. Soup cured everything, she always said.

I tiptoed up the stairs, hoping to make it to my room without disturbing my grandfather or incurring the wrath of Grandma.

"Lucky?"

Crap.

"Yeah, Grandpa?" I pushed his bedroom door open. He was under the blankets. I wasn't sure that I had ever seen him in bed during the day before. "Are you okay? Do you need anything?"

"I'm fine. You know your grandmother." His voice sounded weak. That scared me more than anything else. He looked pale in the light streaming through the window. Grandma hadn't drawn the curtains.

"Are you sure? You look pale. Do you have a cold?" I sat on the bed beside him.

"Just a little indigestion," he promised.

"Are you sure?" I touched his forehead. It was clammy. "Grandpa, maybe you should go to the hospital."

"Lucky, I'm fine," he groused. "I'll just take a nap and be good as new."

"Okay. But I'm going to check on you later," I said. He nodded, closing his eyes before I had even made it off the bed.

CHAPTER NINE

The Walk

Grandpa slept through dinner.

Grandma went up with a tray of soup and freshly baked bread around six o'clock, but brought it back down with her moments later.

"He's asleep, bless him," she said, putting the tray down on the counter and dumping the soup back into the steaming pot before giving it a stir.

"Is he okay?" I asked. She nodded.

"Right as rain," she promised. "He just needs a bit of a rest. I'll take him a tray later," she said.

I heard the front door close before I could register that she was gone. I got up and looked out the window, catching a glimpse of her walking purposefully down the street. It was cold out, but she had left her sweater draped over the arm of her chair.

I headed out after her, taking the front steps two at a time to catch up.

"Grandma? Grandma!" I called at her back. She ignored me. I caught up to her at the end of the street, just as she was about to step into the road. Right in the path of an oncoming car.

"Grandma!" I pulled her back. She spun on me, frowning.

"What?" she asked, rubbing at her bare arms, which were covered in goose bumps.

"Where are you going?"

I pulled my hoodie off and put it around her.

"What are you talking about?" She was trying to shrug off my hoodie.

"It's cold out here, Grandma. Just wear it. Where were you going?"

"I'm not going anywhere!" she shouted.

"Well..." I was at a loss. "You're outside..."

"Of course I'm outside! I'm going home! Can't a woman go home when she wants to?"

"Yeah...but you *were* home, Grandma. You left."

"I don't know what you're talking about," she muttered, tears filling her eyes. I reached for her, but she slapped at my hands.

"I'm just trying to take you home, Grandma," I told her, using the low, calm voice I had heard my grandfather use with her when she had what he called "one of her spells." "Do you want to go home?"

She nodded.

"Okay. We'll go home. Grandpa's probably getting hungry," I told her.

"He had dinner already," she argued.

"Right," I said, knowing he hadn't eaten. "Well maybe a snack then?"

She nodded again.

"I could make some soup," she said. "Soup is good when you're feeling poorly."

"Yes it is," I said, leading her back to the house.

CHAPTER TEN

911

"Lucky! Lucky, help! Oh God, please help me!"

I woke up to screams.

"Grandma?" I was groggy, but when she screamed again, I flew out of bed and down the hall. "Grandma!"

I was in their room in an instant and was met with the horrifying sight of my grandmother standing over my grandfather who was splayed out on the floor.

"What happened?" I asked, falling to the floor and shaking him. "Grandpa!"

"He's sick," she sobbed. "He said he didn't feel right. He grabbed his chest and fell down. He won't wake up, Lucky. Please make him wake up!"

"Grandpa!" I was on the floor beside her, pushing her hands away from him so I could see. Oh god. He was so pale. "Grandpa?" I put my head on his chest. I didn't hear a heartbeat. "Call 911!" I screamed. "Grandma! Call 911! Now!" She nodded and ran from the room. "Okay. Okay. Hang on, Grandpa. You're going to be fine."

I put my hands over the center of his chest and started pressing.

"One, two, three, four…" I counted. Pressing down. Watching for any sign that he was still…there. "Come on, Grandpa. Breathe. Nineteen, twenty, twenty-one…" I kept pressing into his chest, praying to God to feel the thump of his heart under my hands. "Thirty-eight, thirty-nine, forty."

I tilted his head back, pinching his nostrils. "Come on, Grandpa, please!" I breathed into his mouth for a count of two. Waited. Breathed again. "Come on!"

"Is he okay?"

Grandma was in the doorway, holding the phone in her hand. I started compressions again.

"Did you call? Three, four, five…" She nodded. I heard the siren in the background suddenly. "Eight, nine, ten, eleven…. Go let them in, Grandma. I'll stay here. Fifteen, sixteen, seventeen…. Come on, Grandpa!"

The next few minutes were a blur. The paramedics pushed me out of the way, and I ended up standing against the wall, hugging my grandmother while she sobbed into my chest.

"He's going to be okay," I murmured, praying it was true.

CHAPTER ELEVEN
Gone

I closed the door after the last guest had left. We now had a freezer full of casseroles and roasts and a refrigerator full of cheese plates, cold cuts, and enough fruit salad to feed an army.

But it was just the two of us.

It would only ever be just the two of us.

And the house was unbearably empty without Grandpa in it.

The world was unbearably empty.

I looked at my grandmother. She had aged a decade since Grandpa died.

"Do you want me to run you a bath?" I asked her, touching her arm gently.

She started.

"Christina?" she asked.

Shit.

"No, Grandma. It's me. Lucky. Christina's daughter?"

I touched her arm gently. She stared at me for a minute.

"Lucky?"

"Yes, it's me."

We had these little exchanges a few times a day now. She'd forget I was there. Or forget she was. Or forget I was me. Touching her seemed to bring her back. But it was back to a world without the person who had taken care of her for longer than I'd been alive, and it was a void I didn't know how to fill.

"What were you saying?"

"I asked if you'd like a bath, Grandma."

"No thank you, dear."

"Tea?"

She smiled. It was like a light went on and off behind her eyes. When it was off, she thought I was her daughter. Or she forgot where she was. When it was off, Grandma was gone. When it was on, she was right here with me.

"Tea would be lovely. Thank you."

"You go sit down and I'll bring it to you. Maybe there's a movie on TV."

She shuffled off down the hall, her shoulders hunched. She hadn't stood up straight since Grandpa died.

CHAPTER TWELVE

Bacon

The smell of bacon woke me up. Burning bacon. I opened my eyes, nostrils assaulted by the acrid smell. It wasn't even light out yet.

I stumbled down the stairs and into the kitchen. It was empty, but there was a pan on the stove that held something that must have once been bacon. It was on fire.

I blurted out the first thing that came into my head.

"Crap on a cracker!"

It was something my grandfather used to love to say when my grandmother was in earshot. He tended to go a little more risqué when she couldn't hear him.

I grabbed a lid and covered the pan, suffocating the flames.

"What in blazes is going on in here?"

Grandma pushed me out of the way. I hadn't even heard her come into the kitchen.

"Lucky! You could have burned the house down!"

Huh?

"It wasn't me!" I argued.

"Well, we're the only two people here."

Well, that was true. And she *could* have burned the house down. I couldn't watch her every second. Especially not in the middle of the night.

"Come on, Grandma. Let's just go back to bed. It's too early to be awake."

"Someone has to clean this up!" She looked at me pointedly.

"Fine," I sighed. "I'll take care of it."

She yawned and headed for the stairs.

"My goodness, Lucky. Who eats bacon in the middle of the night?"

I clenched my jaw, biting back my words. It wasn't her fault. I wondered though, how many times had Grandpa woken up to a forgotten frying pan? He had managed to keep it all mostly hidden from me. I knew she was forgetful. But I had no idea I had to worry about being burned alive in my bed.

The pan was a lost cause. I trashed it and headed back to bed. But instead of drifting off to sleep again, I stared at the ceiling, wondering if she was going to wander out of the house or cook another midnight snack while I was asleep.

CHAPTER THIRTEEN
Catching Up

Ryan appeared in my doorway while I was trying to distract myself with Netflix.

"You look awful!"

"Gee thanks, Ryan," I sniped at him.

"You need some serious concealer."

"Shut up," I mumbled.

"Did you even sleep last night?" he asked.

"As a matter of fact, I didn't!"

And just like that, the tears were rolling down my face, and I was sobbing so hard I couldn't catch my breath.

I hated crying.

"Shit!" I swiped at the tears angrily with my sleeve.

"What's going on?" Ryan asked, sitting down on the bed beside me and putting an arm around me. His voice wasn't teasing anymore. Somehow that made it worse, and I was suddenly a sobbing mess, crying into his shoulder. "Lucky? What's wrong?"

"Everything!" I was angry. And sad. And frustrated. I couldn't talk to my grandfather anymore. I definitely couldn't talk to my grandma. But Ryan would listen. I knew that.

"Okay." He reached past me for the tissues and handed me the box.

"Thanks." I blew my nose. "Sorry for snotting on your shirt," I said.

"It's fine. It's just GAP."

I laughed at that.

"Lucky, are you okay?"

"No. I miss my grandfather."

He nodded.

"And…"

I hadn't said it out loud…. I wasn't sure I could. I filled my lungs with air and just let it all out.

"I think Grandma's sick. Like, really sick. I knew she was…forgetful…but it's bad, Ryan." Now that the words had started, I couldn't stop them. "Grandpa always took care of her, and I don't know how. I can't watch her every second. She started a fire last night, Ryan. If I hadn't woken up, what would have happened? We could both be dead." I took a deep breath. "And she blamed me for it! She cooked bacon in the middle of the night and then completely forgot about it."

"Jesus. Lucky, you need to tell someone."

"Who? Who am I supposed to tell, Ryan?"

"I don't know. A grown-up. Her doctor. Someone who can help. You can't do this all by yourself."

"Obviously, I know that!" I saw his face cloud. "Sorry. I'm just overwhelmed."

"I know. It's okay. But...have you thought about calling your mother?"

I gawked at him.

"Why the hell would I call her?"

"Don't get pissed off at me, Lucky. You need help. You can't take care of your grandma by yourself anymore."

"I have to! There's no one else. My mother can't even take care of herself. She isn't about to come to the rescue."

"I just...I don't get...how did you not notice how bad she was?"

"What? Are you seriously blaming me?"

"Of course not. But...if she's this bad...did you really not notice?"

"I don't know. I guess...I didn't want to notice," I admitted.

Ryan nodded.

"I get it. I do. But...I think she has dementia, Lucky. She's not going to get any better."

Ryan had just put my biggest fear into words. She really wasn't going to get better. And no matter how badly I wanted things to stay the same, they were changing.

"If I tell someone, they might send her away." My voice was so low I wasn't sure he heard it. "You can't tell anyone, Ryan."

"Lucky…"

"No! You have to promise. I can take care of her! I'll talk to her doctor and figure it out. Just…swear you won't tell."

"But I really think…"

"Swear, Ryan!"

We stared at each other for a long moment. Then the air whooshed out of him.

"Fine. But you're going to have to tell someone eventually."

"I'll tell someone when I can't handle things myself." I nodded. "Promise."

CHAPTER FOURTEEN
A Day Off

I'd spent so much time at home lately that Ryan wanted to treat me to coffee and comics. It's something we used to do once a week, but since Grandpa died, I hadn't managed to make it to The Comic Cellar even once. Grandma was next door with her friend, Mrs. Turner, so I felt pretty confident leaving for an hour or two. And frankly, I needed the break.

We each had a bag full of comics as we sat in the café and ordered.

"Can I see your *Sandman?*" Ryan asked, slurping a Frappuccino smothered in whipped cream and cookie crumbs.

"You need to wipe your hands off before you touch Mr. Gaiman's best work." I shoved a pile of napkins at him.

We spent the next hour or so reading *Spider-Man*, *Deadpool*, and *The Dark Knight*, and arguing about who would win in a fight: DC vs. Marvel version.

"I feel like Deadpool would fight dirty, so he could kick Aquaman's ass," Ryan said.

"Oh my god…is there anyone you think could beat Deadpool?"

"No. Because no one is as awesome as Deadpool."

"Wonder Woman could beat him," I sniped.

"And you think Wonder Woman could beat anyone. She couldn't even beat Aquaman, and he's lame!"

"She can!" I told him. "If Aquaman gets his powers from the ocean, how is he supposed beat Wonder Woman on land?"

"Well…he takes the power with him…" Ryan was floundering. I loved when he floundered.

"He takes it with him? Like in a bottle?" I teased.

"Oh, shut up."

Tara, our waitress *du jour* cleared our cups.

"I'm closing up, guys. Do you want something for the road?"

I literally felt the color drain from my face.

Shit.

I looked at my phone.

Eight o'clock.

We had been gone for six hours.

"I need to go home right now!" I jumped up, stuffing my comics back in the bag, not caring if they got damaged.

"Shit. I'm sorry, Lucky."

"It's my fault. I should have been watching the time. Just…we need to go now!"

CHAPTER FIFTEEN
911 Again

"Can't you drive any faster?" My knee was jittering up and down as I listened to the phone ringing on the other end for the millionth time. "Why isn't she answering?"

"I'm going as fast as I can, Lucky. I'm sure she's fine. Maybe she stayed at the neighbor's for dinner."

"Why don't I have their number? I should have asked for it. Why didn't I ask for it, Ryan?"

"I don't know. We'll be there soon."

He ran a red light, for which I was extremely grateful. I didn't think I could stand sitting at a red light.

"Drive faster, Ryan," I begged. He nodded, and I felt the car surge forward. "Thank you."

Within minutes, we were rounding the corner onto my street.

"What the hell?" Ryan stepped on the gas until we were

fairly flying toward my house and the ring of fire trucks and police cars surrounding it. Smoke was curling upward, and I could see the glow of flames though the front window.

"Oh my god. Grandma!" I screamed, jumping out of the car before he had even come to a stop. "Grandma!" I ran for the house, but before I could get there, an arm grabbed me around the waist, lifting me off the ground. "My grandmother's in there!" I screamed, clawing at his arm. "Let me go!"

"It's okay, miss. Your grandmother is being checked out by the paramedics. She's right over there."

I could barely see through eyes half blind with tears and smoke. I stopped fighting him.

"Where? Where is she?"

"I'll take you," he said, loosening his iron grip.

Grandma was perched on the back of an ambulance, wrapped in a gray blanket. She looked unbelievably small.

"Grandma!" I ran to her, throwing my arms around her and hugging her tightly. "Are you okay?"

"I'm fine." She patted my back awkwardly through her blanket.

"What happened?" I asked, pulling away and pushing her hair out of her eyes.

"How should I know?"

"What...what do you mean?"

"I was reading and someone started a fire. I saw smoke so I went outside and that nice man over there," she pointed at the firefighter who had stopped me from running inside the house, "brought me over here and gave me a blanket."

"Your neighbor saw smoke and called 911. I know it looks bad, but the damage is really just in the kitchen," the firefighter said.

My heart sank. She must have been cooking again. If I hadn't been late getting back, I could have made her something to eat.

"Your father is going to be very upset, Christina," my grandmother said. I saw the firefighter exchange a glance with the paramedic.

"I'm Lucky, Grandma," I told her wearily.

"You *are* lucky," the paramedic said. "The fire could have been much bigger."

"No. My name is Lucky," I told her.

"Who's Christina?" the firefighter asked.

I considered lying briefly. But I was just too tired.

"She's my mother."

"Does she live with you?" he asked.

"No. It's just me and my grandmother."

"And your grandfather? Where is he?"

I glanced at my grandmother.

"He died."

The paramedic led me away from the ambulance, out of earshot of my grandmother.

"How long has your grandmother been confused?" she asked.

"I don't know…for a while, I guess."

"And has she done this before? Left the stove on?"

"Yeah. Once. But I was here so it wasn't a big deal. She

just forgets sometimes. I was late, and she must have gotten hungry...." I trailed off. I was digging a hole that was too big to get out of.

She nodded, not unkindly.

"I think she needs to be assessed, Lucky. I'd like to take her to hospital and have a doctor examine her. Do you have someone you can stay with? Can you call your mother?"

"I haven't seen my mother in years," I told her. "Can I come to the hospital with her?"

"No, I'm sorry. You can follow us though. But I think you'd better call your mother. You'll need an adult to make decisions if she can't make them for herself."

"All right. I'll call her. But don't expect much."

I glanced at Ryan, who had come up to stand beside me. He nodded. "I'll drive you there."

CHAPTER SIXTEEN
Exam Room Seven

They wouldn't let me ride with Grandma even though I begged and she threatened them with legal action if they didn't let me. I don't know what she had in mind, but it didn't work. Thank goodness Ryan was there to follow close behind the ambulance.

"What am I supposed to say to my mom?" I asked him. "I don't even know if I have the right number for her."

"You can stay at my place. My aunt and uncle won't mind," he said.

"Thanks. But I think they want someone who can make medical decisions or whatever. And I'm a minor. My mother is the only…family we have." I spit the word out. She wasn't family. She didn't want anything to do with either of us.

"Do you want me to come in with you?" he asked, pulling up outside the main entrance.

"No. I don't know how long I'll be here."

"Well you can't stay at your place, so call me when you need me to pick you up." He leaned over and gave me a hug.

"Okay. Thanks."

"It'll be all right, Lucky. They'll get you and your grandmother the help you both need."

I nodded, but I had a bad feeling. It felt like there was a rock in my stomach or something. Grandma had gotten worse, and now that she really had set the house on fire, I didn't know what they'd do with her. Or me.

I waved at Ryan and felt the rush of cool as the sliding doors to the hospital whooshed open. There was a buzz of energy as soon as I walked in, with doctors rushing around and patients shuffling by, supported by nurses. There was a desk in front of me with a harried-looking nurse trying to reason with someone on the phone.

"I can't give you a diagnosis over the phone, sir. You have to come in. Yes, I know it takes a long time to be seen when you come into the emergency room, but unless it's an emergency, you can wait to see your own doctor in the morning. I don't know if it's an emergency, Sir. You'd need to see a doctor for that. No, I can't put one on the phone. Yes, I'm sure. Then you'd better go to the emergency room, Sir. Okay. Good-bye."

She set the phone down and shook her head.

"Excuse me?"

"Yes?"

"An ambulance just brought my grandmother in. Can you help me find her?"

"Name?"

"Daisy Robinson."

She clicked some keys.

"They just brought her in…. She's probably not in your system. I think they wanted to check her out…to be sure she's okay. We had a…bit of a fire."

"Ah! Yes. I saw her come in. She's down the hall with the doctor. Go left. Exam room…seven."

"Okay. Thanks."

It was easy to find. I could have found it with my eyes closed anyway, when I heard her voice from all the way down the hall.

"I don't want to answer any more of your questions. I just want to go home!"

I knocked and walked in on a doctor and a nurse trying to block my grandmother from leaving.

"Ma'am, you can't leave yet. We have to make sure you're all right first."

"I'm fine! Lucky, tell them."

"Grandma, just let them check you out, okay?" I put an arm around her shoulders and guided her into a chair.

"I want to go home!" she whined.

"We will," I soothed, pulling the other chair toward her so I could keep a hand on her arm. "Just let them do their jobs, Grandma."

The doctor nodded at me. She looked like she had been on her feet all day and wanted nothing more than to sit down herself. But she smiled kindly at my grandmother and examined her to make sure she hadn't breathed in too much smoke or anything. She kept up a steady barrage of questions while her nurse took notes.

"So you forgot that the stove was on, Mrs. Robinson?"

"No. Someone else did," Grandma said stubbornly.

"But you were home alone, weren't you?"

"I don't know. I can't remember now."

"Have you ever left the stove on before, Mrs. Robinson?" the doctor asked gently.

"No. Maybe."

"Do you find that you forget things, Ma'am?"

"I'm old. Of course I forget things!"

"Grandma, they're just trying to help," I said, hoping to calm her down.

They asked question after question. Some of them, my grandmother answered, some she shrugged off, and others she got downright belligerent about. I was exhausted.

Finally, they let Grandma lie down for a bit and led me out into the hallway. The doctor smiled at me kindly. Sadly.

"I'm sure you're aware that your grandmother is suffering from dementia, Lucky."

I nodded. I didn't want to hear the words...but I knew.

"When can I take her home?" I asked wearily.

"Has she forgotten things on the stove before? Wandered off? Forgotten your name?"

"Well...yes. But I've been taking care of her, and we're doing okay. Mostly."

"You can't take care of her by yourself. Is there someone else who can help?"

"No. It's just the two of us."

"She mentioned her daughter. Your mother?" she asked.

"Yes. But we haven't seen her in years. She's an addict."

"Is there anyone else? She's either going to need significant help at home or she'll have to go into a care facility."

"She can't go into a…a facility!"

"Do you have someone you can stay with, Lucky?"

"I can stay with my friend, Ryan."

"I mean long-term."

"Long-term? What do you mean? Just let me take her home and we'll be fine. I'll keep a closer eye on her. It was because I was late getting home!" I swiped at my eyes angrily.

"And what about the next time you're late? I'm sorry, but someone has to make some tough decisions."

"I'll make the decisions!"

"I'm so sorry, but you can't. You're a minor. You should call your mother. We'll keep your grandmother here until she can be assessed further and a long-term care plan can be worked out."

"How long will that take?" I asked.

"It's hard to say. It depends what's causing her dementia. She'll get a room for now and we'll start trying to help her." She reached out and touched my arm. I wanted to smack her hand away but I knew, deep down, that it wasn't her fault. "Call your mother. Tell her she needs to come as soon as she can."

I nodded as she turned and walked away. I hoped suddenly that my phone would be dead so I could put this call off, but the battery was at eighty-three percent. I scrolled until I found a number under the name CHRISTINA. I dialed and waited.

"Hello?" said a voice I assumed was my mother's, but which I hadn't heard in so long, I couldn't be sure.

"Christina Robinson?" I asked.

"Yes."

"It's Lucky. Your daughter."

CHAPTER SEVENTEEN
Mommy Dearest

ME:	My mother is coming
RYAN:	Rly?
ME:	I can't make decisions re gma
RYAN:	Y not?
ME:	Too young
RYAN:	Do u want me to pick u up?
ME:	No. I have to wait. I'll txt u ltr
RYAN:	Kk. XO

I had walked around the entire floor three times so far. There wasn't much to see. They had moved my grandmother to her own room, and she was sleeping, thanks to a dose of Ativan that had calmed her down considerably. The doctors left me alone, and I was just finishing my fourth lap when I saw the doctor standing outside Grandma's room, talking to a woman in a black suit and what Grandma would have called "sensible heels." Her lipstick matched the startlingly pink blouse she had on, and it was smudged slightly.

"Lucky, this is Cynthia. She's from Children's Aid."

"Why?"

"Why what?"

"Why is Cynthia from Children's Aid here?" I asked.

"Because you're a minor, and we're required to call and make sure you're being cared for."

"I'm fifteen. I can take care of myself."

I suddenly heard the staccato clack of stilettos in the hall and somehow just *knew* they belonged to my mother.

She looked considerably older and much more weathered, but otherwise, she was basically the same. A mess who had bleached her naturally dark hair until it looked like straw. She had way too much makeup on and a skirt that I instinctively wanted to pull down to cover a few more inches.

"I'm lookin' for room eighteen. Are you the doctor?" she asked the only person outside the room wearing a lab coat.

"I am. You must be Christina." They shook hands, and I cringed at the ragged fingernails with their chipped red polish. It looked like she had chewed them off.

"I'm Cynthia," said Cynthia from Children's Aid. My mother nodded and shook her hand as well. She looked at me expectantly.

"And you are?" she asked, holding out her hand. Was she serious? Jesus.

"I'm Lucky. You know...your daughter?" My voice was dripping ice.

"*Oh, my god!* It's been a minute since I've seen you, hasn't it?" she brayed. "You're all grown up. What do you need me for?" she asked the doctor. "Lucky's grown."

"Your daughter is fifteen," Cynthia from Children's Aid told her. "She's still a minor."

"Oh, right. Of course."

"Your mother has dementia. She's going to need help, and Lucky can't take care of her by herself. Are you able to stay with them? Help out?" Cynthia asked. She didn't look very hopeful.

"I mean...I can stay a minute, but my boyfriend, Dan? He has a gig in Thunder Bay, and we're going to road trip..." She trailed off, perhaps realizing that we were all looking at her in disbelief—and in my case, disgust.

"She can't live with just me!" I shouted, forgetting for a second where I was. "She needs another adult to help make decisions, and unfortunately, you're the closest thing she has. She needs you!" I paused. "I need you." I hated to admit it, but it was true. I didn't want Grandma going into some care facility, and I didn't want to end up on the street or whatever.

"Well...how much does it pay?"

"How much...I'm sorry?" Cynthia looked completely shocked. And I imagine it took a lot to surprise her, in her line of work.

"What do I get for staying and helping? Do I get a check?"

The doctor was speechless. Cynthia looked like she was

trying not to yell at my mother. I was livid, but not even a little bit surprised.

"You're her daughter. And you're Lucky's mother. You don't get paid for that, Miss Robinson."

"Right. It's just that I've kind of been on the road with my boyfriend—he's a musician—and I'm not sure I can stay here right now. I'm not really the mom-type." She snorted with laughter at this. Like deserting your kid and your mother was something hilariously funny to her.

"I understand that. I do. But your mother needs you," the doctor told her. "Maybe you'd like to see her? Talk it over with her? She's asleep now but when she wakes up?"

"Oh, sure. For sure. I mean, yeah. I'll just go grab a smoke and then come back. I can catch up with Lucky while we wait for her to wake up."

"Of course," the doctor said. I kept my mouth shut. I had seen this particular number before.

"All right then. I'll be right back." She turned and clickety clacked back down the hall without a look back at me.

"See?" Cynthia from Children's Aid smiled. "I think she understands the severity of the situation."

"Right. I'm sure she does," I said, watching my mother's retreat and knowing for absolute certain that she wouldn't be back.

CHAPTER EIGHTEEN
A Wake-Up Call

My neck hurt.

The blue chair upholstered in the scratchiest fabric known to man didn't make much of a bed. I was draped across it, my neck dangerously kinked, trying to get a little sleep.

"Lucky?" Cynthia from Children's Aid was back.

"Umm...yeah?" I moved my head this way and that, trying to work out the kink that had settled into it.

"Why are you still here? Where's your mother?" she asked, looking around the room as if my mother might be hiding in a corner somewhere.

"I assume she left." I yawned.

"What do you mean, she left?" Cynthia frowned. She looked exhausted. I pitied her. How could she not have seen my mother for what she was?

"Look, Cynthia...with all due respect, my mother wasn't

going to step up and take care of anyone. She can't even take care of herself. If there was nothing in it for her, she wasn't going to stick around."

"Well you can't sleep here." She gestured at the blue chair I had been dozing in.

"I can call my friend Ryan to come and get me. I'll just stay with him." I shrugged.

"Lucky, unfortunately I can't let you do that," she said.

"Why? I've stayed with them before. It's not a big deal."

"You're a minor. Children's Aid is responsible for you now until we figure out what's happening with your grandmother or until we can find a legal guardian for you. Do you have any other family you can call?"

"No. There's no one. So what does that mean?" I asked, not liking where this was going.

"Well…I'll have to find you a foster home to sleep in tonight. Probably for the next couple of nights until we can figure out your grandmother's situation."

"Foster care? But I can stay with Ryan! I don't want to go into foster care!"

"It's just temporary. You can't stay with a friend, Lucky. There are protocols for this sort of thing."

"The sort of thing where I'm not allowed to go home?" I demanded.

"I'll do the best I can. And I can try to call your mother again too. Maybe she'll change her mind."

"Right. I'm sure she'll suddenly grow a conscience. Where am I staying?"

"I have a couple that takes kids in when there's an emergency situation. I'll call them. In the meantime, we can go pick up some of your stuff."

"That's it? I have no say in what happens to me?"

"I'm sorry. I really am," she said.

"Right. Well...not as sorry as I am."

CHAPTER NINETEEN
Fosters

Everything smelled like smoke. The fire had been contained in the kitchen and hallway, but the entire house smelled like smoke. And just...wetness. A dampness that I knew I'd be smelling on my clothes and skin for a long time. The fire department had hosed everything down well, and I wasn't sure how we'd ever clean it all up again when Grandma came home and we moved back. *If* she came home.

I shook my head. I wasn't even going to consider that.

What was I supposed to pack? I was hoping I'd be back home before I had to change clothes too many times, but Cynthia told me to pack enough for a week, just to be safe.

I grabbed a bag and stuffed some clothes into it. My laptop, phone, and chargers. My sketchbook. Some pencils. My iPad. The comics Ryan and I had bought but hadn't gotten around to reading yet. I looked in the closet for a hoodie and saw a pile of sweaters that Grandma had made for me. She had knit me a sweater for every single birthday and Christmas since I was a kid. There were three sitting in a pile on the top shelf. Two, I was sure, were getting too small, but she had just recently given me the third. It was a soft, mossy green color that reminded me of spring. I touched it, thinking of her spending evenings in front of the TV with her needles, and packed all three even though I probably wouldn't wear them.

"Ready?" Cynthia asked, looking up as I trudged down the stairs.

"I guess so."

"Good. All right. The Wilsons are waiting for you."

I nodded, trying to picture "The Wilsons" in my head. What kind of people took kids that weren't theirs into their homes?

We drove for a while...way out of my neighborhood.

"How am I going to get to school?" I asked.

"The Wilsons homeschool their kids," Cynthia said.

"Wait...I don't want to be homeschooled! I want to go to my own school!"

"They don't live in your district, Lucky."

"I don't care! I want to be with my friends!" I argued.

"I'm really sorry. I am. But that's not possible. We don't have a foster family available in your district. The Wilsons were the only ones that could accept you tonight."

"Accept me? Like I'm a delivery from Amazon or something? Jesus. I have friends I can stay with!" I seriously considered jumping from the car and running for it.

"You know it doesn't work that way. I'm sorry, Lucky. I really am. But this was the only option."

We pulled into the driveway of a modest, two-story house. As Cynthia turned off the engine, a couple walked out and stood on the porch, arms around each other. The Wilsons, I assumed. The porch light shadowed them a little, but I could see that he was big and burly; she was small and blonde.

"Well, here we are," Cynthia said. "Come on and meet your foster family."

I felt a chill—an actual chill—as I opened the door of the car and stepped out. Someone was watching me from an upstairs window, and my instinct as I walked toward the couple standing on the porch was to run. Run fast and run far. Run back to my grandmother.

CHAPTER TWENTY
The Wilsons

The man came down the stairs and grabbed my backpack out of my hand before I could stop him. I mean, he had a good foot and a half on me, so I probably couldn't have stopped him even if I wanted to. But there was something about letting that bag go that made me feel like I was losing a battle.

The man—Mr. Wilson—held out his other bear-like hand to me.

"You must be Lucy," he said, pumping my hand enthusiastically. "I'm Robert Wilson. And this is my wife, Mary."

Bob and Mary. Of course those were their names.

"It's Lucky," I told him.

"Sorry?" He looked confused. Not an uncommon reaction to my name.

"My name. It's not Lucy. It's Lucky," I explained.

"Oh! Sorry about that. Lucky. I've never heard that one before. Is it short for something?" he asked.

"Nope. Just Lucky," I told him. He nodded, pumping my hand a few more times before releasing me.

"Are you hungry, dear?" his wife—Mary—said, smiling. She looked nice enough. They both did. But all the niceness in the world wasn't going to make me want to stay with these people.

"No. Thank you. I'm just tired."

"Lucky has had a long day. I'm sure she'd like to get some sleep. I'll leave you with Bob and Mary, Lucky. I'll check in on you tomorrow."

And just like that, she was gone. You'd think Cynthia from Children's Aid would stick around long enough to get me settled in, but maybe she had other kids to save tonight.

"I'll show you to your room," Mary said. "You'll have it all to yourself. It's just us and our son, Robert Jr., right now."

Ah. The boy in the window. I had assumed he was a foster kid. She took the backpack from her husband and led me inside.

"Okay. Thanks."

The first thing I noticed when we walked into the front hall was the cross. Now don't get me wrong. My grandparents had a cross or two. They went to church. They believed. But this was a CROSS! In capitals. It was easily several feet tall. And it had a pretty scary looking Jesus staring down at me with what looked like condemnation. So it was going to be *that* kind of house. I kind of felt like Carrie in that Stephen King book. I wondered if Mary was going to tell me they were all going to laugh at me or mention my dirty pillows. Seriously. If you haven't read the book, at least see the movie. Ryan and I had seen it eight times at least. I was even Carrie for Halloween one year.

There was music playing softly from somewhere down the hall. It was a hymn I had heard many times. Mary hummed along quietly as she led me upstairs. I saw a face peering out of a slightly cracked open doorway.

"Hi," I called out, but the door slammed shut without a response. Mary acted like she hadn't seen this. Weird.

"Here you go." She opened a door and put my bag inside. I walked into the smallish bedroom and nodded. It was fine. Nothing fancy. Nothing at all that set it apart from any other room. The walls were bare except for a small gold cross above the bed. The furniture was white, and there was what I assumed to be a handmade quilt on the bed.

"Thanks. Ummm...goodnight?" She was still standing there smiling. More and more Stephen King-like by the minute.

"Goodnight, Lucky. We're happy to share our home with you," she said. I nodded, and she finally left, closing the door behind her.

I looked around. There was a dresser, but I was hoping I'd be out of here tomorrow or the next day at the very latest, so I didn't bother unpacking. I put my backpack on the bed and opened it. The first thing I saw was a picture of the three of us. Me, Grandma, and Grandpa, arms around each other, smiling widely at the beach a couple of months ago. I held it up, staring at the life that had collapsed completely in the last month.

CHAPTER TWENTY-ONE
Breakfast

I slept surprisingly well, considering the completely foreign environment. I didn't have a clock in the room so I had to find my phone to see what time it was.

10:45.

There was a text.

RYAN: Hey. U ok? Let me know where u r so I can come c u

I had texted him the night before just to let him know what was going on. I still felt like things would work themselves out and I could go stay with him.

ME: I don't know the address. I'll txt u ltr. Pretty sure I'm in Castle Rock

RYAN: LOLZ

He was as big a Stephen King fan as he was a comic book nerd. I loved that about Ryan.

I changed into shorts and a T-shirt and wandered out to find the bathroom. It was right beside the bedroom, between it and the son's room. I pulled my hair back into a ponytail, washed my face, brushed my teeth, and put my stuff back. I could smell bacon and eggs and maybe...waffles? My stomach growled. The last thing I had eaten was a chocolate bar from the vending machine at the hospital.

Mary was at the counter doing dishes when I came into the kitchen.

"Good morning, sleepyhead," she chirped. "We don't usually sleep in, but I thought you could use some rest."

"Yeah. Thanks."

"Would you like some breakfast? I kept it warm in the oven for you."

My mouth was watering.

"Thank you!"

"You sit. The plate will be hot." She gestured toward the table, where I eagerly pulled a chair out and sat down. "Those shorts are awfully short," she said mildly.

Huh? "I'm...sorry?"

"There's a teenaged boy in the house, dear. I'd appreciate it if you covered yourself up a little more."

Mary was still smiling but it was forced. She put the plate in front of me, but I had lost my appetite.

"Oh. Okay," I managed. "I guess I can change into something else." I poked at a piece of bacon.

"Maybe before you eat?" she suggested, still smiling.

"Oh. Sure."

I stood back up and headed upstairs. I didn't feel like breakfast anymore. Especially not with Mary judging my perfectly acceptable shorts.

CHAPTER TWENTY-TWO
Class in the Kitchen

I came back downstairs in jeans. I figured my T-shirt didn't break any commandments or anything. Mary was at the table with her son when I walked in. I couldn't help but notice that my breakfast had disappeared.

"Lucky, you're looking better."

Better?

"Sure," I said. I mean…what was I supposed to say? Her son was looking at me oddly. I was completely covered, so my clothes weren't to blame for this.

"Great! This is my son, Bobby. You're in the same grade so you can do your work together. Why don't you have a seat and we can get started."

I forgot she homeschooled. Oh. This was going to be weird.

I sat beside her son who still hadn't said a word to me.

"Hi," I said, smiling at him.

He flushed and looked away.

"Bobby, say hi to Lucky," Mary instructed him.

"Hi," he muttered.

Okay then. Off to a great start. Clearly we were destined to be BFFs.

"I thought we'd start with English today..."

The next few hours passed by, literally, at a snail's pace. Mary's method of teaching was to read out loud from a textbook, including study questions. In every subject. It was excruciatingly boring, but she was nice enough, and once we started talking about history, even Bobby joined in.

I learned we only had half days with the expectation that we'd work on assignments ourselves, so that wasn't so bad. By lunchtime my stomach was growling so loudly that even Bobby grinned. Robert Sr. wandered in for lunch. He was a contractor apparently and was working close enough to home that he could come back for meals. He was bigger than I remembered. Kind of lumbering and gruff. But he smiled kindly and asked how my morning was as he sat down to tomato soup and grilled cheese sandwiches with us. Much as I wanted out of here, I had to grudgingly admit that they seemed fine.

Bobby came out of his shell around his father, and they spent the entire meal talking about a car they were fixing up together. I ate my lunch in silence, eager to go back upstairs to text Ryan and try to call Grandma. She must be worried about me.

"Do you think I could go visit my grandmother today?" I blurted out.

Robert glanced over at me.

"I think they probably want her to get settled in before you visit," he said.

"But she's going to be worried about me," I told him. "If I could just go for a quick visit, just to let her know I'm okay?"

"Not today. But soon, all right?" He nodded, signaling that the conversation was over.

"Well, when is Cynthia coming back?" I asked.

He looked at me again, clearly annoyed this time.

"Probably not until the end of the week. Now if you're done, you can help clear the table," he said before turning back to Bobby and resuming their scintillating conversation about engines.

I stood up without another word and took some of the plates to the sink. Robert had dropped his napkin—yes, they used real napkins here—and I stooped to get it for him. I glanced up and caught him looking down the gaping neck of my T-shirt. I grabbed at the material, holding it against my chest. He met my gaze and held it, challenging me to say something. What could I possibly say?

"I'm going to start on my homework," I said, turning quickly and heading upstairs, feeling Robert's gaze following me from the room.

CHAPTER TWENTY-THREE

Double Stuf or it Doesn't Count

I tried calling Ryan but there was no answer. I thought he might be asking Thomas out today, so he was probably stressing out and had his ringer off, planning what he was going to say. It was funny. Thomas clearly liked him but Ryan still thought he wasn't good enough for people. That was his parents' doing.

I tried Grandma next. It took a couple of different receptionists before I was connected to her room. I almost cried when she answered.

"Hello?"

"Grandma? It's Lucky." My voice broke. It all hit me at once. Losing Grandpa. The fire. Grandma in the hospital. And me stuck with a foster father who was turning out to be kind of a perv.

"Lucky girl! Are you okay?"

Leave it to Grandma to forget that she was the one in the hospital.

"Yeah, Grandma. I'm fine. I'm staying with a family in...I don't know. The west end, I think? Just for a while. Just until you're back home. Are you all right?" I asked.

"I'm fine, sweetheart. Bored out of my mind. Can you bring me a book? Or a crossword?"

"Yeah, Grandma. I'll bring you something to do," I promised.

"And maybe some cookies or something. They gave me Jell-O for dessert here. Jell-O isn't a real dessert!" she huffed.

I laughed. Her hatred for Jell-O was well-known in our house.

"Okay, Grandma. I'll bring you some Oreos or something."

"Double Stuf or it doesn't count," she said. My eyes burned. That was one of Grandpa's sayings. Oreos weren't worth it if they didn't have extra icing in them.

"Double Stuf or it doesn't count," I agreed. "I miss you, Grandma."

"I miss you too, Lucky girl. I can't wait to see you." I could hear the smile in her voice.

"I'll be there as soon as I can," I said. I hung up and pulled up the transit app on my phone. It would take a while, but if I left now, I could get back into the city and down to the hospital before visiting hours were over. I pulled my wallet out. I had forty dollars and a transit card that was good until the end of the month. I could get her some books and cookies and still have money left over in case I needed something.

I could hear Mary and Bobby in the kitchen doing the dishes. Hopefully Robert was gone. I figured I could get down the stairs and out the front door without them seeing me. I tiptoed down, heart stopping at every squeak of the stairs. I went slowly, knowing I could be caught and have to explain where I was going after Robert told me I couldn't go see Grandma. But finally I made it to the hall and sidled my way to the front door. One more glance behind me and I was out, running up the street toward a bus stop and toward my grandmother.

CHAPTER TWENTY-FOUR
The Visit

I decided to add some flowers to the growing pile of things I picked up on the way to see Grandma. I was glad I did. Her room was okay. It wasn't horrible or anything. But there was no color to it. No life. It reminded me of my room at the Wilsons. No personality.

"Do you like them, Grandma?" She was fussing over the flowers. Arranging and then rearranging them in the water jug that we had repurposed.

"I love them, Lucky. Thank you!" She smiled widely at me.

"Are they treating you well?" I asked.

"Yes. Everyone's very nice. Did you bring Oreos?"

"Of course!"

She dug into them, taking three and setting them down on the tray in front of her. She picked the first cookie up and took it apart. She licked the icing, just like Grandpa used to do. I had never seen her eat an Oreo that way before.

"Hmm. Now I get why he ate them like this," she mused, sticking it back together before biting into it. I smiled gently. I missed him so much. "Are those people nice? The one's you're staying with until I come home?" she asked.

I thought about telling her the truth. I really did. But she couldn't help, and I didn't want to add to her stress with stories about my possibly pervy foster father. It was only for a little while anyway. I took a deep breath.

"Yeah, they're great," I lied.

"Wonderful! Have a cookie." She pushed the package toward me. I took one and pulled it apart, just like Grandpa.

"I brought you a couple of books." I dug into the bag again. "I've got crosswords too. And a word search book." I handed them to her, and she leafed through one of the novels eagerly.

"Thank you, Lucky girl. I watch the TV, but they don't have all the channels, and I swear, I need to exercise my brain or I'll go crazy in here." She grinned. I didn't know how to respond. She wasn't crazy…but it felt like something in her brain wasn't connecting. It's why she forgot to turn the stove off or thought that Grandpa was just out running errands. She was fine today, but who knows if she'd even recognize me tomorrow.

"No problem, Grandma. I have to get back. But I'll come visit as soon as I can."

"Okay, sweetheart. I love you." She put her book down and held out her arms for me. I leaned into her and held on tight.

"I love you too, Grandma."

CHAPTER TWENTY-FIVE
Trouble

It was getting dark when I got off the last bus and walked toward the Wilsons' house. I was glad I had seen my grandmother, and I had pretty much forgotten that I had been told I couldn't go see her.

At least until I walked in the front door and all hell broke loose.

"Where *have* you been?" Mary shrieked before I even had time to kick off my shoes.

"I went to visit my grandmother," I told her, pretty calmly all things considered.

Robert appeared behind her.

"I said you couldn't go," he told my breasts.

I tried to catch his eye and failed.

"Yeah, well…she's my grandmother, and she needed me."

I tried to walk past and go up to my room. Or the room I

was borrowing anyway. Unfortunately, the Wilsons had other ideas and moved to block my escape.

"Look, I was going to call and let you know where I was, but I don't have your number. I didn't think I'd be back after dark. I'm sorry, but she needed me. I had to go." I figured that would smooth things over a little.

"You're not getting off that easy," Mary said. "Our rules are for your own good!"

"You have a rule that says I can't visit my grandmother?" How was this such a big deal? "I'll make sure to let you know next time I'm visiting," I told her, trying to ease my way past.

"You need permission!" she screamed. Robert patted her arm, pulling her out of the way.

"All right. I think Lucky knows she made a mistake and can see that we worry, and next time she'll make sure she asks for permission. Isn't that right, Lucky?"

"Yeah. Sure." I nodded and slid through the space that was now open in front of me.

"No dinner!" Mary called at my back.

I ran for it before she could come up with something more creative. Like being tied to a chair or something. This was insane. How was I supposed to live with people who couldn't understand that I needed to be with my grandmother? I closed the bedroom door and flopped down on the bed. Between the hymns and the homeschooling and the creepy father-figure who kept staring at my chest…I needed to get the hell out of here.

ME: Ryan, you've got to get me out of here.
RYAN: What's going on?

I spent the next hour rant-texting Ryan and trying to figure out how to live with these people until I could get back home. I was yawning by the time I said goodnight and headed to the bathroom to brush my teeth and get ready for bed. Bobby's door was closed. I realized he was the only one who hadn't bothered to confront me when I walked in and felt a rush of gratitude. He might be the only halfway normal person in the house. Except that he couldn't say a word to me without turning bright red.

The door to my own room was ajar. I walked in and found Robert standing by my bed with his back to the door.

"Can I help you?" I asked warily.

He turned. He had a plate in his hands.

"I thought you might be hungry. Mary and I differ when it comes to punishments." He smiled. He was actually looking at my face for a change. He handed me the plate, which held a sandwich—ham and cheese—a couple of cookies and an apple. "I don't believe teenagers should skip meals," he explained.

"Oh." I was genuinely shocked. Both by the fact that he had brought me food and that he wasn't being skeevy. "Thanks. That's really nice of you."

He set the plate down and smiled again.

"No problem. I want you to be happy here, Lucky." He nodded and walked past me, completely non-creepily. "Oh. And don't tell Mary I snuck you food, okay? I don't want to get in trouble." He winked and retreated, closing the door behind him.

Well, that was odd.

I took a bite of ham and cheese and grabbed my phone to text Ryan.

ME: You're not going to believe this!

CHAPTER TWENTY-SIX

Another Day, Another Lesson

"Good morning, Lucky!" Mary trilled as I came down the stairs the next morning, appropriately dressed and not as hungry as she probably thought I was, thanks to her husband.

"Good morning." I nodded at Bobby, who was already reading a textbook. He nodded back and only turned slightly pink. Baby steps.

"You must be starving! I made pancakes." She plopped a plate down in front of me. They smelled heavenly. Ha. Heavenly. I should have said that out loud.

"Thank you." I cut a huge bite of fluffy pancake and was about to stuff it down my gullet when Mary interrupted in that sugary sweet way of hers.

"Aren't you forgetting something?" she asked, eyeing me like an insect.

"Sorry?" The fork was right there! My mouth was watering.

"Don't forget to say grace, dear."

Oh, for crying out loud.

"Oh. Sure. Of course." I lowered the forkful of pancake regretfully and closed my eyes. I talked to God in my head sometimes, but I didn't appreciate anyone telling me I *had* to pray. I thought quickly…ummm…. *Please keep my grandmother safe and let me go home soon…amen.* I opened my eyes. Mary was still staring at me. "Okay then," I said, gulping down the mouthful of slightly less mouthwatering pancakes before she could make me take communion or something.

Once breakfast was over, Mary started our lessons. I had a hard time paying attention. She read in a monotone and then just made us answer the questions in the textbook. There had to be more to homeschooling for most people than just working our way through a textbook. It was enough to put you to sleep!

I was just dozing off when she closed the book with a slam. I jumped.

"There you go. Now go through the questions, and we'll review tomorrow. Don't forget the quiz on Friday!"

I rolled my eyes and caught Bobby looking at me. *Busted!* I expected him to rat my disrespect out to his mom, but he grinned and stacked his books in a pile.

I followed him up the stairs.

"Boring, isn't it?" he whispered. Was this a trap?

"Yes! God! I mean, jeez! How do you stand it?"

He turned his head and smiled.

"I just tune her out. I'm way ahead of her, but I let her do her thing and work on other stuff in my head."

"Really?"

He nodded.

"Yeah, I passed her in the text about a year ago. I just didn't have the heart to tell her. I'm doing university-level stuff, but I just get books out of the library and work on my own and let her read whatever she wants."

I laughed out loud. I had misjudged this kid.

"Don't tell her though," he said.

"Don't worry. Your secret is safe with me."

CHAPTER TWENTY-SEVEN

Marvel vs. DC

I was thinking that the Wilsons—for the most part—weren't so bad. I mean, if I had to stay *somewhere* then I guessed this place wasn't completely terrible. They were okay if you could get past the hymns and being forced to say grace and the homeschooling. Bobby had some comics that we were trading back and forth, and as long as I stuck to the rules, things went pretty smoothly.

I still wasn't sure about Robert. He was nice. As nice as the other two. But there was just something…off…about him. It was the way he looked at me when he thought I wasn't paying attention.

"If you could only read one comic book series for the rest of your life, what would it be?" Bobby asked. He was lounging on the floor of my room, sorting through a pile of comics and dividing them into Marvel and DC.

"Excellent question!" I nodded approvingly. Weird as this house could be, I actually felt like Bobby was a friend. I thought about inviting Ryan over for one of these comic book debates. He'd love this. "Ummm... *Ultimate Spider-Man*. Definitely. You?"

Bobby looked toward the door, then back at me.

"*Deadpool*," he whispered.

"Your mom lets you read *Deadpool?*" I blurted out.

"Shhhhh!" He gestured toward the open bedroom door. "Of course not. My friend Dan collects them. I read them at his house. Don't tell my mom!"

"Absolutely not!" I promised. "My friend Ryan *loves Deadpool.* Have you seen the movies?"

"Yeah." He grinned. "Laughed my ass off."

"Right! Let me guess. You watched them at Dan's?"

He nodded, laughing.

"You're a secret badass, Bobby," I told him, handing him a *Daredevil* comic to add to his Marvel pile. He was smiling in a way I hadn't seen since I started staying with them. I suspected this was the real Bobby. I kind of liked him. I definitely had to invite Ryan over.

"Bobby? Time for bed." Mary's voice preceded her up the stairs. Bobby's face changed instantly, and he immediately started shoveling his comics back into the milk crate he stored them in. "Bobby?"

"Shit!" he whisper-screamed. "Help me!"

"Oh. Okay." I knelt down beside him and picked up a bunch of comics. "In there?"

"Yes!"

"Bobby, where are you?"

She was coming down the hall now, and it suddenly occurred to me that it wasn't the comic books he was trying to hide. It was the fact that he was in my room. I started shoveling them into the crate faster.

"Just go," I whispered. He nodded frantically.

"What are you doing in here?" Mary was standing in the doorway. Bobby flew to his feet as I piled the rest of the comics in the crate.

"I…ummm…" Bobby looked at me desperately.

I stood up.

"I borrowed his comic books and he came…to the door… to get them. And I dropped the crate so he came in to help me."

Mary studied me for what felt like ages, then turned to her son.

"Is this true?"

"Yeah. Yes. Yes, Ma'am."

She was studying him now. She looked like an owl, eyeing its prey. She nodded brusquely.

"All right then. Off to bed, Bobby. I'll be in to say goodnight in a second."

Bobby took the crate and with one desperate glance back at me bolted from the room. Mary closed the door behind him and turned to stare at me with her owl-like gaze.

"Lucky, Bobby is a very…special boy. He's not like other boys his age."

I had no idea what she was talking about. He seemed pretty normal to me.

"Okay."

"He's not worldly like you are. He doesn't have experience with girls like you."

Wait...girls like me? This woman clearly thought I was some kind of slut.

"Look, you've got the wrong idea, Mary. We were just looking at comic books. I swear."

"I hope that's true. Bobby doesn't need anyone leading him into sin."

"I'm not. I promise." What did that even mean?

"All right. Well...goodnight, Lucky."

She was gone before I could figure out what to say. She had basically just called me a whore. Which I wasn't. Not even close. I liked her son but definitely not like that! I was tempted to go after her but what was the point? Grandpa always said that changing someone's narrow mind was next to impossible.

I got ready for bed instead. Maybe tomorrow she'd see I wasn't nearly as bad as she thought I was.

CHAPTER TWENTY-EIGHT

An Unwelcome Visitor

I had weird dreams that night. I was hanging out with Batman and Spider-Man and trying to explain to them why they shouldn't be together in the same dream. I told Spider-Man I had his back. He told me to be careful. He said I was in danger.

"From who?" I asked Spidey.

"Don't trust anyone," he told me.

"Well...what kind of danger am I in?"

"The worst kind. The very worst. Just be careful, Lucky."

Before I could say another word, Spidey was gone, flinging himself into the sky on a thread.

"Wait! Who do I have to be careful of?" I yelled. I pushed a piece of hair out of my face. It tickled. Like there was something working its way through my hair.

A spider! It had to be a spider! I shrieked and flailed my way awake. The first thing I noticed was Robert sitting beside me on my bed. The second thing was that he had his fingers entwined in my hair.

"What…what are you doing?" I pulled away from him. He had the nerve to smile at me. Smile!

He reached for me again, and I flinched away.

"Stop it!"

He laughed softly.

"You were having a nightmare," he said. "I just wanted to make sure you were all right."

"By playing with my hair?" I retreated as far away from him as I could get, pulling the blanket up around me as far as it would go.

He took it as an invitation and started getting into the bed with me.

"What are you doing?" I demanded.

"I'm just trying to comfort you," he wheedled back, sliding under the covers beside me. I felt his leg press against mine and that was all I needed.

I fairly flew out of bed, flinging myself over him while trying not to touch him. I got across the room and threw the door open. I was shaking.

"Get. Out!"

"Oh, come on." He grinned, his eyes roaming over me. I was reminded suddenly that I was wearing only a thin tank top and a pair of boxers I should have thrown out a year ago.

I crossed my arms over my chest.

"Get the fuck out of my room or I'll tell your wife you got into my bed!" I waited for him to apologize. To get out of the bed and beg me to keep my mouth shut. Instead, he laughed. He actually laughed!

He lurched off the bed and sauntered over to me like we were visiting at church or something. But he stopped in front of me and grabbed the front of his pajama pants, rubbing himself through the thin material while staring at my body.

"Who's going to believe you?" He smiled.

CHAPTER TWENTY-NINE

A New Look

I couldn't sleep after Robert left. I had seen enough police procedurals and read enough books to know what happened in some foster homes. But I didn't expect it from a family that played church music all day and prayed more than I was comfortable with. But as soon as that thought popped into my head, I remembered Ryan's family. How they had treated him when he came out to them. I felt a chill go down my spine and I shivered, remembering that sometimes people aren't what they seem to be.

Every time I started to drift off, I felt Robert's fingers in my hair and his leg pressed against mine, and my eyes would pop open again. I kept expecting him to be leaning in the doorway staring at me.

I tossed and turned. I flailed. I twisted myself into knots in the sheets. And I felt his hands in my hair until I couldn't stand it another second.

I opened the door a crack and peered out. The hallway was empty, as far as I could tell. I slowly opened the door farther, willing it not to creak, and tiptoed down the hall to the bathroom. I flipped the switch and closed my eyes against the sudden blaze of light. I found scissors in the medicine cabinet and stared at my reflection for a second, doubting I could go through with it. At least until I felt his hands on me again. Then, without a second thought, I grabbed a lock of hair and with a snip, watched it fall into the sink. I grabbed another bunch of hair and lopped it off. With each snick of the scissors, I felt a weight lifting off me. And when I had finally cut enough of it off that I didn't feel his hands on me anymore, I stared at myself again. I'd fix it tomorrow, but for now? I liked it. I looked like a badass. I looked like someone who wasn't going to put up with any shit from a creepy foster father.

There was one more thing I needed to do before I could sleep.

The stairs creaked as I crept down them. I knew if anyone was still awake, they'd hear me wandering down to the kitchen, but I was past caring. The moonlight streaming through the window lit up the room enough for me to see without turning on the lights. I stepped toward the butcher block on the counter and pulled out one of the knives. It was satisfyingly heavy in my hand. Mary kept her knives razor sharp.

With a firm hold on the knife, I felt stronger going back upstairs. Braver. I slid it under my pillow and climbed back into bed. Now I could finally sleep.

CHAPTER THIRTY
Saturday

"He did WHAT?" Ryan was screaming into the phone. "Lucky, you need to tell someone. Call that woman from Children's Aid. There is no way you can just let that go. He could have raped you!"

"I know, Ryan. I'm just going to avoid him. I won't be here forever."

"You don't know how long you'll be there. Your grandmother might not get better, Lucky. What if you're stuck with that guy and you don't tell anyone what he did? What if he tries it again?"

"Then he'll be sorry," I blustered, sounding more confident than I felt.

"What do you mean?"

"I took a knife from the kitchen. If he tries it again, I'll use it."

"Oh, come on, Lucky. You're not going to attack him, are you?"

"Not if I don't have to," I said.

"Just be careful, okay? We won't get to have that comic book date if you get sent to juvie."

"I'll be careful. Promise."

"Call me later."

"I will."

It made me feel a million times better to hear Ryan's voice. Somewhere out there beyond the walls of The Wilsons' House of Insanity, my old life still existed.

I ran my hands over my head. I had borrowed an electric razor from Bobby and now had a pretty awesome haircut. Bobby had watched from the doorway until he couldn't stand it any longer and grabbed the shaver from me.

"Why are you shaving your head?" he had asked curiously, shaving down one side and leaving the other so that it rested at chin-length.

"I just want a change," I told him. I had no idea how he'd respond if I told him it was because I couldn't stand the memory of his father's hands in my hair. It was an exorcism. I felt reborn when we were done.

I walked down the stairs toward the kitchen with trepidation. I had no idea if I was going to see Robert lording over everyone at the breakfast table, and I had no idea how I was going to react if I did. But he wasn't there. I breathed a sigh of relief as I sat down to a plate of waffles and a bowl of fruit salad.

"So is your friend still coming?" Bobby asked.

"What's this?" Mary set a glass of orange juice in front of each of us, then jumped back. "What on earth did you do to your hair?"

"I cut it. My friend Ryan is coming. Remember, I asked if he could visit?" I reminded her.

"Right." She nodded. "Ryan. I forgot." She puttered off toward the sink, still tutting about girls looking like boys or something.

"So when is he coming?" Bobby asked. I got the impression he didn't get many visitors. Or have many friends. Which was too bad because he was actually pretty cool.

"Tomorrow. He's bringing a bunch of comics and a DVD for us to watch," I told him.

"A DVD?" Bobby glanced toward his mother's back.

"Don't worry. I told him it had to be Wilson-friendly," I grinned. He smiled gratefully. He may like *Deadpool*, but he certainly wasn't going to watch it in the comfort of his own home.

"All right, you two. Finish up so we can get started on our science work." Mary put a pile of books down on the table as we shoveled the last bites into our mouths.

CHAPTER THIRTY-ONE

Nightmares

I had put the knife back that morning so Mary wouldn't notice it was gone. Having effectively avoided Robert for the entire day—it was pure luck he had been away at a church meeting at dinnertime—I actually felt pretty good. But not quite good enough that I didn't double back to the kitchen later that evening to slide the knife out of the butcher block again.

Just in case, I told myself, slipping it underneath my pillow before setting my newly shorn head down.

I was asleep within seconds, dreaming I was home with Grandma and Grandpa. Dreaming we were sitting in his boat, waiting to reel in a big one for dinner while we talked about books and movies and his favorite carrot cake that Grandma was making for dinner.

I woke up when the bed shifted.

I woke up to Robert breathing his boozy breath in my face. Church meeting, my ass!

I scooted back toward the wall, pulling the knife out from under the pillow so violently that I felt it slice through the pillowcase. I held it up, touching the razor-sharp tip against his Adam's apple.

His eyes opened so wide, they were more white than blue.

"Don't move," I hissed. He looked like he was about to say something, but the prick of the knife so close to his jugular seemed to have shut him up. "I used to go fishing with my grandfather," I told him, my voice far calmer than I felt. "He taught me to clean a fish before I learned to read. I can gut a trout in sixty seconds. I doubt you'd take much longer."

He swallowed hard, and I watched the tip of the knife poke into his skin slightly.

"You wouldn't dare," he whispered.

I laughed. "Try me," I told him. "I don't know how many foster kids you've messed with in the past, but I'm not about to let some middle-aged pedophile molest me in my bed. If you don't get out of my room, I'm going to scream loud enough to wake up your wife and your son, and you can explain to them what you're doing trying to climb into my bed."

He got up slowly, so slowly, while I got up with him, still holding the knife in front of me. He backed out into the hallway, and I didn't look away from his lizard eyes for even a second. As soon as he was out the door, I closed it and leaned against it. I had been operating on pure adrenaline, but now that it was over, I couldn't even make it back to the bed.

CHAPTER THIRTY-TWO
Revelations

I got up the next day, ready to go down and tell Mary what her creepy husband had been up to in the night. Then I'd call Cynthia from Children's Aid and let her know exactly who she had left me with. I could either let this keep happening or I could tell someone and maybe prevent other girls from being placed with a man who probably had gotten away with things I didn't even want to think about.

I shuddered and pulled my hoodie around me as I walked into the kitchen. Mary was sitting at the table, her hands around a cup of tea. She looked up when I walked in.

"Sit down," she said.

"Okay. Listen, there's something I want to talk to you about," I began. God, this was going to suck.

"Oh, I know exactly what you're going to say," she said, her eyes narrowing.

"You do?"

"My husband told me everything."

I was gobsmacked. He told her?

"What…did he tell you?" I asked carefully, pulling out a chair and sitting across from her. She met my eyes, and I realized suddenly that she hated me.

"My husband told me how you threatened him with a knife." She spit the words out at me like venom.

"Did he tell you why?" I asked, struggling to keep my voice calm and not scream YOUR HUSBAND IS A PEDOPHILE at her.

"He told me that you demanded he give you money," she said. "And that if he didn't, you'd make up disgusting lies about him."

"What? That's not what happened!" All semblance of cool was gone. I wasn't surprised. Of course, he wasn't going to admit what he had done. But I felt attacked all over again.

"Oh, he told me everything," she insisted.

"Everything?" I laughed. "You think that's everything? He tried to get into my bed!"

"You're a liar!" she screamed. Bobby came in then, his face white. "Go back to your room!" she yelled at him. He was gone before I could say anything to him.

"I'm not lying. And I'd bet my life it's not the first time he's done something like that."

"You're a filthy liar. I've called Children's Aid. Go pack your bag. You're leaving as soon as she can get here."

"I didn't do anything!" I yelled back. I didn't even want to be here, but I'd be damned if the reason I was being sent away was on me. "He came into my room when I was sleeping. He touched me. He got into my bed! All I did was protect myself."

"You're evil! Get your bags and wait outside. I won't have evil in my house." She turned away, dismissing me. I stood up, shaking, staring at her back.

"I've got news for you, lady. The evil in your house was here long before I came."

I left the room before she could say another word. I had nothing left to say. I headed up to pack my stuff before Cynthia came to take me away.

"Are you okay?" Bobby poked his head out of his bedroom as I passed. I turned and looked at him, not entirely sure he wasn't going to attack me next.

"Yeah. I have to pack," I told him.

"I know."

I nodded and moved toward my room.

"It wasn't your fault," he called out. His words stopped me cold. I turned and looked at him.

"What do you mean?"

"I know you didn't attack him. You're not the first girl my mother has sent away."

"Then say something!" I begged.

"He's my father! No one would believe me anyway."

"They're sending me away!"

"I know. But there's nothing I can do, Lucky."

"Please, Bobby! You have to say something. What about the next girl?"

He shrugged, leaning against his doorway like all his strength had left him.

I shook my head and turned my back on him. I got it. I did. But that didn't make it okay.

CHAPTER THIRTY-THREE
Pick Up

Bobby's bedroom door was closed and Mary was nowhere to be seen when I came down with my bag. I brought my stuff outside and sat down on the front steps until Cynthia pulled up in her silver Prius.

She waited until I got into her car and buckled my seatbelt before she lit into me.

"What were you thinking?" she asked, pulling out of the driveway, squealing her tires as she took off down the street. "The Wilsons are a good family! Do you have any idea what I had to do to get you into their house with no notice? And you attack Robert? With a butcher knife? What were you thinking, Lucky?" she repeated. I stared at her.

"You're not even interested in hearing my side?" I demanded. "You're just going to assume I'm the one who did something wrong?"

She looked startled but only for a second.

"I've known the Wilsons for years," she told me. "They're one of my best foster families. You were lucky to be placed with them!"

"Lucky?" I laughed. I actually laughed. It was so incredibly ridiculous how blind she was. "So it was lucky that Robert decided to climb into my bed in the middle of the night?"

"That's not true," Cynthia said.

"It is. And you need to make sure you don't send another kid in there."

Cynthia looked over at me and then signaled. She pulled into a gas station and turned the engine off.

"Tell me exactly what happened," she said.

I did. I told her about the hymns and the forced prayers. I told her about how Robert had stared at me. And the way he put his hands in my hair while I slept. And how he got into my bed. I told her why I had defended myself with the kitchen knife. She looked me in the eye and nodded but let me talk and didn't interrupt once.

"Do you believe me?" I asked her. Might as well cut to the chase, I figured.

"I...I don't know what to believe," she admitted. At least she was honest. And she wasn't dismissing me outright. "I've placed countless kids with them. No one has ever complained."

"No one?" *How is that possible?*

She shook her head.

"So? What now?" I asked.

"Now? I take you to another foster home. And I suspend the Wilsons until I can investigate."

"Really?" Truthfully, I had expected her to just side with them. Because none of what had happened to me or my grandmother was fair. Why should this be?

"Yes. I promise. And if anything like that happens to you again…call me. Day or night. I mean it, Lucky."

"Okay."

She started the car again and took off, her forehead creased in a frown.

"I forgot to tell you," she glanced at me suddenly, "they're moving your grandmother to a care facility."

"What? Why didn't the hospital call me? Someone should have let me know!"

"I'm sure they're going to call. But I was at the hospital anyway so I checked in on her. I got the address. You can call her later." She reached over into the bag on the console between us and pulled out a piece of paper. I took it from her.

"Sunset Seniors?" I choked. "Is that where they send people to die?"

"No! Of course not!"

"What's their tagline? 'Sunset Seniors: Where Seniors go for the Twilight of their Lives?'"

Cynthia laughed out loud, which made me giggle.

"I'm sorry. I don't mean to laugh. It's actually a really nice place. They specialize in dementia and Alzheimer's care. They have special programs for their residents and all kinds of therapy. You can visit as soon as she's settled. They'll even help make arrangements for packing her things and selling her house."

"Why would they sell it?" I felt my heart pounding in my throat. "They can't do that, can they?"

"I assume they need to speak to your mother."

Oh, shit.

"Why would they need to talk to her?"

"She's your grandmother's closest relative."

"*I'm* my grandmother's closest relative! What has my mother ever done except desert me? Or hurt my grandparents? I've been there. I took care of her when my grandfather died. My mother walked out and left us over and over again. She takes everything and leaves. That's what she does."

Cynthia nodded.

"Okay. Well…maybe your grandparents have a will or a directive or something. Someone needs to go through your house."

"I'll do it. I mean, if these people let me. I can go back and help pack her stuff up."

"You'll like them," Cynthia promised.

Sure, I thought. I was almost positive she had said that about the Wilsons too.

CHAPTER THIRTY-FOUR
Another Family

I was taken into a house that looked a lot like the last one (minus all the religious paraphernalia) and up a flight of stairs that seemed to hold the exact same number of steps, into a bedroom that looked startlingly like the one I had just left. The walls were beige and devoid of any decorations. The single bed was covered in a nondescript blanket. There was a dresser and a night table holding a lamp. It was as soulless as a hotel room.

I had just set my backpack down on the bed when my phone pinged.

RYAN: I did it!
ME: Did what?
RYAN: I asked Thomas out!
ME: OMG! Tell me everything!
RYAN: When can I come over? I can fill you in then.

Oh shit.

ME:	I'm not there anymore. They moved me.
RYAN:	Bcuz of the pedo?
ME:	Kinda. I'll tell you later.
RYAN:	U ok?
ME:	Ya. I'll txt l8tr
RYAN:	Kk

I had been looking forward to seeing Ryan, and now that wasn't happening. And they were moving Grandma. And selling my house maybe. I just wanted to crawl into bed and disappear. My own bed. Not this one, with its hard mattress that crackled when I sat down.

I stared at the wall, trying to decide if I should go downstairs or take my stuff out and put it in a drawer. It would all fit into just one. I took a deep breath and scrolled through my phone until I found my mother's number. She was the last person I wanted to talk to. I'd actually be perfectly happy to never see her again.

It rang hollowly, and I pictured her rolling over in some crack den, completely strung out with her wannabe rock star boyfriend in a drugged-out stupor beside her.

"H'lo," I heard her say. It sounded like I had it about right.

"Christina?"

"Mmm."

I took that as a yes.

"It's Lucky."

There was a pause during which I was fairly certain she was trying to remember who I was.

"Your daughter?" How many people could she possibly know named Lucky?

"Hiiii!" she squealed like a kid. This was getting weird.

"So, I wanted to talk to you about Grandma's house. I need to go and pack up some of her stuff and take it to her."

"She's in the hospital," she said.

"Yes. Thank you. She's not though. She's going to be staying in a care facility for a while," I told her. "Until she's ready to go back home."

"She's not going home. The doctor said so." God. She was infuriating. It was like talking to a petulant child.

"Yeah, well…the doctor is wrong. She's going to get better and go home. So until then, we can't do anything with the house. Okay?"

"If she's not coming home, someone gets the house?"

"I don't know," I blew out a deep breath of complete frustration. "It depends if Grandma and Grandpa had a directive or something. But the point is, she's not going to be in that place forever, and when she gets out, she'll need to go home. Do you understand?"

"Yeah. I guess. But why are you telling me this?"

She sounded suspicious. That wasn't good.

"Because you're family," I told her through clenched teeth.

"Yeah," she said and hung up on me. I wasn't sure if I had done more harm than good. If no one had even called her about the house, then I had just planted the seed in her head that she might now be a home owner.

CHAPTER THIRTY-FIVE

Home #2

I was staring out the window at a block of houses that all looked exactly the same, on a street that could have been in any suburb in Canada. I couldn't have told you where in the city I was if you had held a gun to my head.

If I was even in the city at all anymore.

Someone knocked gently at the door.

"Yeah?"

The door cracked open and the foster parent du jour, Sarah, poked her head in.

"Hi, Lucky. Are you all settled in?" She looked at the backpack, still clearly crammed full of my stuff.

"Oh. Yeah. I was going to unpack later."

She nodded and smiled.

"Dinner's ready in ten. You're off the hook for chores,

being that it's your first night. My husband, Edward, just got home, so wash up and come on down and meet everyone."

"Okay. Be right there."

I dug around in my backpack until I found the framed photos of Grandma and Grandpa, and I put them on the night table. This wasn't home. It would never be home. But at least there was one thing that felt familiar in the room now.

The kitchen was a hotbed of activity when I walked in. There were two boys setting the table, while Sarah laughed at something one of them had said. I stood in the doorway and watched them, not wanting to intrude.

"Hi," a soft voice came from just behind me. I spun around. After Robert, I didn't like being surprised by anyone sneaking up on me. The guy behind me jumped back, pushing his glasses up his nose. "Sorry. I'm so sorry. I didn't mean to startle you."

"It's okay," I assured him.

"You're Lucky, right?"

I nodded.

"Interesting name. Any idea where it came from?"

I wasn't really interested in explaining the origins of my name to a complete stranger. People tended to look at you pretty strangely when they found out your druggie mom decided to name you Lucky because she hit the jackpot at the casino one night.

"Nope. No idea, actually."

He smiled and held out his hand.

"I'm Edward." He had a firm handshake for such a slight guy. He looked like an academic. Glasses and a tweed jacket. "We're happy to have you join our family."

"Thanks. But I'll be going home as soon as my grandmother is better."

He nodded.

"Well, you're welcome here until then. Guys! Did you say hi to Lucky?"

The chaos around the table stopped as everyone turned to stare at me. I waved awkwardly at them.

"Ummm…hi."

One of the boys nodded. The other came over and stood in front of me.

"'Sup? I'm Jake."

"Hey. Lucky."

"Is that short for something?"

"Nope. Just Lucky," I told him. He nodded.

"Cool name." He smiled. "That's Charlie. He doesn't talk much."

"I talk," the other boy said. "Sometimes."

"He does," Jake said. "But only if you happen to be into the same nerd stuff he's into."

I looked over at Charlie and looked him up and down.

"DC or Marvel?" I asked him. His face lit up, and he met my eyes for the first time.

"Marvel! All the way." He grinned.

"*That* is the right answer," I agreed. "Have you been reading the new Spider-Man?"

"Nah. I don't really have the money to buy many." His face was pink.

"I have some of the new ones. You can borrow them," I told him.

"Seriously?"

"Oh lord. There are two of them," Jake sighed. Edward and Sarah were watching us, smiling happily. And, it's important to note, Edward was *not* looking at me with any kind of unhealthy interest. He cleared his throat.

"Dinner looks ready, guys. Go wash your hands. And Lucky?"

"Yeah?"

"I'm a Superman fan, myself."

I laughed.

CHAPTER THIRTY-SIX
From Famine to Feast

Dinner was an interesting change from what it had been at the Wilsons' house. For one thing, no one forced me to pray before I ate. And there was laughter. Lots of it. The two foster kids seemed to actually enjoy being around Sarah and Edward. And Sarah and Edward listened with great interest to Charlie and Jake.

The food was different too. Mary Wilson's cooking was… okay. Nothing memorable. Meat and potatoes with very little seasoning to spice it up.

But Sarah clearly loved to cook. She had filled the table with bowls of mouthwatering Indian food. Butter chicken. Piles of naan on a plate. Basmati rice. And a vegetable curry that was full of cauliflower and chickpeas and smelled absolutely heavenly.

"This is amazing!" I shoveled another forkful of chicken into my mouth. My stomach was full, but I couldn't stop eating.

Sarah looked pleased.

"Thank you, Lucky!"

"Make sure you leave room for dessert." Edward smiled.

I groaned. *Dessert too?*

"She made carrot cake," Jake said.

"I helped!" Charlie elbowed him.

"Yes, you did." Sarah smiled gently at him. They genuinely liked each other. It was kind of surprising after my first experience with a foster home.

I helped clear the dinner plates despite being exempt from chores for the night. I sat back down and accepted a piece of amazing looking cake.

"So, I was hoping I could visit my grandmother," I blurted out. I didn't know how to ease into it.

Edward looked up from his piece of cake and nodded.

"Can you figure out the bus route?" he asked.

"Yes." I was surprised he didn't ask any questions. Clearly he already knew about her.

"Then you can go after school. Just be home for dinner," he said.

"I will. Thanks." It was that simple. No pleading or arguments or sneaking out.

I dug into my dessert. It was almost as good as Grandma's carrot cake.

CHAPTER THIRTY-SEVEN

Fitting In

I wasn't close enough to my old school to go there, but anything was better than being homeschooled. I drifted through the halls and found my classes with the help of Charlie, who magically appeared at the door at the end of every class to take me to the next one.

The kids were mostly friendly enough. The teachers were helpful. But I just wanted to get through the day and go visit Grandma.

"I don't have lunch until later," Charlie told me, stopping at the door to the cafeteria. "But Jake should be in there somewhere." He wandered off to chemistry and left me standing inside the door, holding my brown-bag lunch and looking for somewhere to sit.

"You look lost." Jake appeared beside me suddenly. "Come on. You can sit with me." He led me over to a table full of the kind of kids who never gave me the time of day at my old school. You know the type. The jocks and the cheerleaders, neither of which I had ever been. The shining stars of the school. The mostly blonde girls and the muscle-bound guys. "Hey guys. This is Lucky. She's the new kid at Sarah and Edward's place."

The guys, most of whom looked like athletes, gave me a thorough once over, mumbling greetings. One of the girls said hi, but the others stared at me in way I could only describe as hostile.

The redhead at the end ignored me completely and called out to Jake.

"Jake! Come sit here. I saved you a seat." He smiled but sat beside me. *Shit.*

"I'm good over here, Elyse. Thanks though." *Double shit.*

She was glaring at me openly.

"Girlfriend?" I asked, digging into my lunch bag. Sarah had packed a pretty fantastic-looking turkey sandwich, homemade chocolate chip cookies, and a fruit salad.

Jake laughed. "No."

"Does she know that?" I asked, biting into the sandwich. It had brie and thin slices of Granny Smith apples in it. "Oh my god, this is amazing," I moaned. I caught the redhead rolling her eyes and nudging her friends. I turned back toward Jake and tried to ignore them.

"So? Are you settling in?" he asked, biting into his sandwich. "Wow. This is fantastic."

"I know, right? Yeah. I guess. Charlie meets me after every class to help me find the next one."

He laughed, which wasn't lost on Elyse the redhead. She was scowling pretty openly at me now. Jake didn't seem to notice.

"Yeah, he's a good kid."

"How long have you been staying with Edward and Sarah?"

"Ummm...about a year. Charlie's been there for three years, I think."

"Really? Wow. And...they're cool? No...issues?"

"Nope. They're really nice. I was in another home before this one, and the parents there weren't anything like them."

"Yeah. I was with another family too. Briefly. It wasn't a good situation."

He nodded.

"I know what you mean. Lots of foster homes are a nightmare. But Edward and Sarah are great."

"Really? No skeletons in the closet?" I asked, using one of my grandfather's favorite terms.

Jake laughed. "Nah. I mean, they have rules, and they're pretty strict about them."

"Like what?"

"Normal stuff. No stealing. No lying. No fighting. No going out without telling them where you are. Treat everyone in the house with respect. Do your chores."

I was relieved. They were the same rules my grandparents had at home.

"Oh. Okay. I was expecting...I don't know. Three hours of church every week or something," I said.

He raised an eyebrow.

"You did live in a weird home, didn't you?"

He had no idea. It wasn't the religious aspect. I could have dealt with that. I had respect for everyone's beliefs. But having to fend off a lecherous foster father wasn't what I'd call normal. Telling Ryan about it was one thing. He was my friend for life, and I knew I could tell him absolutely anything. But Jake got it. I didn't have to share any details or explain how vulnerable I had felt. How helpless. He already knew. We smiled at each other, and I caught Elyse glaring at me over his shoulder. Again. God, couldn't she just back the hell up?

"Yeah," I admitted, pointedly ignoring Elyse and focusing on Jake. "I miss home a lot."

He nodded.

"I'm sorry about your grandfather," he said softly. I guess Cynthia from Children's Aid had filled everyone in. "And your grandmother."

"Thanks. I mean...she'll get better though. And then I'll be able to go back home."

Jake looked at me like he knew something I didn't. I wasn't about to get into my grandmother's situation in the cafeteria.

"So...how did you end up in foster care?" I asked. *Oh shit. What if you weren't supposed to ask that?* "I'm sorry! You don't have to tell me," I quickly amended.

"No, it's fine. My mom couldn't take care of me. She's got some...issues. She's trying to get it together, but I'm better off with Edward and Sarah."

"Yeah, I get that," I said, thinking of my own mother's "issues."

"And Charlie's been in care since he was a baby. His mom

gave him up." He smiled tightly. "What about you? I mean...I know you lost your grandfather and your grandmother is sick... but how did you end up with them?"

"Oh, you know," I told him, "Junkie mom who'd rather get high than feed her kid. My grandparents raised me. Grandma is the only family I have left."

Jake was smiling softly at me, and I was finding it hard to look away. Or come up with something to say. Or breathe. Thankfully, Charlie appeared suddenly and shoved his way up to the bench. He tossed his lunch bag onto the table.

"What did I miss?" he asked.

"Nothing," Jake assured him. "I'll walk Lucky to her next class. You can eat," he said. "Okay with you?"

"Sure," I agreed, standing up and gathering the remnants of my lunch.

"I'll meet you after," Charlie called out.

"Okay. Have a good lunch. Nice meeting you all," I called out to the rest of the table. They waved or nodded. One called out, "See ya," and another said, "You too." But I'm about ninety-five percent sure I heard Elyse say something that sounded suspiciously like "whore." I wanted to respond. I literally had to bite back the words. But then I thought about seeing Grandma after school. I could already see the look on her face if I told her I got into a fight on my first day of school. And I could hear Grandpa's voice clearly in my head.

"Don't ever let anyone tell you you're not enough, Lucky. You come from a long line of strong Indigenous people. Do them proud."

With Grandpa's words reverberating pretty loudly in my head, I smiled at Elyse and her friends in what I hoped was a friendly manner, then turned and followed Jake out of the cafeteria.

CHAPTER THIRTY-EIGHT
Care Facility

It took three buses and a subway ride to get to the place where they had taken my grandmother. The second the doors swung open, I was greeted by an atmosphere I could only describe as calming. There was classical music tinkling away in the background, and I immediately caught the scent of what I thought was lavender and vanilla in the air. The lights were comfortably set—not too bright, not too dark—and there was a fresh arrangement of flowers on the front desk.

"Excuse me." I waited for a receptionist in muted colors to finish typing something into the computer. She looked up and smiled widely.

"How may I help you?" she asked in a soft voice.

"Hi. I'm here to visit my grandmother. Daisy Robinson?"

"Just one moment," she said, typing into her computer again. "Okay…I'm going to have someone come and get you," she said. "Just have a seat." I nodded and walked over to a cream-colored sofa. It looked like it cost more than all of the furniture we had at our old house.

ME:	I'm at the care facility. You should see it. It's like a Four Seasons
RYAN:	You've never been to a Four Seasons
ME:	True. But it's how I *imagine* a Four Seasons
RYAN:	Ha. Give her my love
ME:	I will.

"Miss Robinson?" I looked up from my phone, nodding. "I'm Nalda. I'm your grandmother's nurse."

"Hi." I shook her hand, which was stronger than I would have given her credit for.

"I'll take you to see your grandmother in a second, but I thought I'd better talk to you first," she said.

"Okay."

"Your grandmother is having a bad day," she told me.

"Oh. Okay. Well, I'm sure I can cheer her up."

"No. Sorry. I should have been clearer. Alzheimer's patients can have bad days sometimes. She's confused today. You should be prepared for that. She doesn't remember where she is."

"Alzheimer's? But…she hasn't been diagnosed…" I trailed off.

"The doctors have diagnosed her."

"Oh. I…see. Okay." My heart sank. She had been fine

at the hospital when I visited. I figured she'd be ready to go home soon.

"So if you're ready, I'll take you to her room. She has a few of her things, but if you could bring things that remind her of home, I think it would help her adjust."

"All right. I'll try."

She led me down a long hall, past a big room where men and women sat together playing cards and chatting happily. This place looked so much nicer than the hospital. I bet Grandma was cleaning up at poker or whatever they were playing. She loved cards but wouldn't gamble real money. Wherever my mother had picked up her gambling addiction, it wasn't from her parents.

"Right in here," Nalda said, gesturing at the door.

"Okay. Thanks." I knocked and waited.

"Who's there?" I recognized my grandmother's voice but not the tone. She sounded shaky. Uncertain. And my grandmother was neither shaky nor uncertain. Grandma was strong.

I opened the door and poked my head into the room. She was in bed with the lights out except for a bedside lamp. At four o'clock in the afternoon. Her hair was disheveled, and she looked frail, like the bed was swallowing her up. I stepped inside, closing the door gently behind me.

"Grandma? Hi."

"Who's there?" her reedy voice called out. *Who's there?* I mean...I did call her Grandma.

I moved into the light being cast by the lamp.

"It's me, Grandma."

"Christina?" She squinted at me. I shook my head gently and perched on the bed beside her, taking her hand.

"No, Grandma. It's me, Lucky."

She studied me for a long moment while I prayed she'd recognize me. She smiled suddenly.

"Lucky girl!"

"That's right, Grandma." I leaned over and kissed her papery cheek that usually smelled like the powder she used. Today she just smelled like she had been tossing and turning all night and needed a shower. "How are you today?" I asked.

"I want to go home!" she said, her voice quivering.

"I know, Grandma. So do I." I hugged her hard. "But you need to let them take care of you."

"They took me!"

"Who did?"

"I don't know! These people. They took me out of the hospital and they made me come here. I just want to go home, Lucky."

"You're in a place where they can take care of you, Grandma."

"I can take care of myself!"

"I know," I soothed. "But you need help, Grandma."

"You help me," she said.

I was struggling to keep her calm and not burst into tears. I wasn't a big crier by any stretch of the imagination, but I suddenly felt like I was the grown-up. And I still needed her to tell me that everything was going to be okay.

"I know I do. But you need doctors to help you."

"I'm not sick," she grumbled.

I felt tears prickle behind my eyelids.

I hugged her again to avoid telling her that she was, in fact, sick.

"Don't let them keep me here," she whispered.

I buried my face in her hair that needed to be washed and let the tears fall.

CHAPTER THIRTY-NINE
Problems?

I barely got back in time for dinner, and I missed my turn setting the table.

"I'm so sorry!" I dropped my backpack on a chair and rushed into the kitchen. "It took forever to get back. I'll clear the table and do the dishes," I promised the boys.

"Don't worry," Jake whispered. "I bribed Charlie with a Mars bar."

"I would have done it anyway," Charlie added, grinning.

"What?" Jake shoved Charlie playfully.

"Hey, you offered the Mars bar. What was I supposed to do? Say no?"

"Dinner's ready," Sarah called out, pulling a lasagna out of the oven. It smelled heavenly. "How was your visit, Lucky?" she asked, carrying dinner to the table.

"Okay, I guess. Grandma was having a bad day," I admitted, shoveling in a mouthful of lasagna.

"I'm so sorry. It must be really hard seeing her like that," Edward added.

"Yeah." I looked down but not fast enough to miss the sympathetic look between Edward and Sarah. "I mean...she's usually fine. But she had a bad day. I guess she didn't understand why she couldn't go home." The words flew out of me before I could stop them.

Sarah nodded knowingly.

"My mother has dementia," she said. "So I know how you feel."

"Really?" She hadn't mentioned it before. "Does she live in a home?"

"Yeah. A great one that helps her do as much for herself as she can. She has friends. She has amazing caregivers who take care of her on her bad days."

"Yeah. This place looked really great."

"She's at Sunset?"

I nodded.

"That's a terrific place. She's in good hands, Lucky."

"I was hoping I could go back to our house and take some of her things to her."

"I'll take her," Jake volunteered. "I mean, if it's okay for me to take the car."

"I'll help," Charlie offered.

"Can they?" I asked.

"Sure," Edward said. "Just..."

"Be back for dinner!" the three of us yelled, laughing. Sarah and Edward joined in. We felt like a family in that moment.

"And how was school?" Sarah asked. *Ugh.* I thought quickly while I chewed. I wasn't sure if I should tell her how the girls at the table had treated me. It seemed unimportant in that moment. And I didn't want to say anything about Jake's friends. I settled for passivity.

"It was okay."

"No problems?"

"Problems? Umm. Nope. No problems."

"That's good."

I wasn't lying exactly. No one had been rude to my face. Just behind my back. Okay, it was kind of to my face. But they were at the other end of the table. Maybe I was lying a little.

"Yeah. All good," I assured her.

Liar.

CHAPTER FORTY
Just Smile

When the alarm I had set on my phone went off the next morning, I actually felt well rested for the first time since the fire. I wasn't worried about Edward coming into my room. I didn't wonder if my grandmother was being taken care of. I actually managed to turn my brain off long enough to get some sleep.

It was a pretty great feeling.

I got up and stretched, mentally going through my backpack full of clothes and trying to put together an outfit. Most of my clothes were dirty, but I had a pair of jeans, and I could wear one of the sweaters Grandma had knit for me. They were getting small, but I figured I could get a little more wear out of them before I had to retire them for good. I looked around the room and wondered if Sarah would let me put up some pictures or something. It was like staying in a hotel. Nothing, other that my meager belongings, actually indicated I lived here. I wondered if Sarah and Edward would mind if I brought some of the things from my room at home. Just until I moved back. I looked around and pictured my things scattered around the room, making it feel more like me.

Making it feel more like home, I amended.

I walked downstairs with a smile, planning to talk to Sarah, but only Charlie and Edward were downstairs.

"Where's Sarah?" I asked, grabbing a banana.

"She had a doctor's appointment. Are you ready?" Charlie asked, shouldering his backpack.

"Yeah. Let's go."

Jake wasn't a morning person, according to Charlie, so he filled a travel mug with coffee and brought it with him. Charlie kept up a steady stream of chatter to fill the quiet. I enjoyed him. It was like having a little brother.

A little brother who still insisted on meeting me after every class.

"You don't have to walk me to my classes," I assured him after third period. "I know where I'm going now." He followed me to my locker so I could grab my lunch.

"I know. But I figured you might like the company." He grinned, walking with me to the cafeteria.

"I do," I agreed. "Thanks."

"No problem. Hey, there's Jake." He waved. "See you later?"

"You bet," I told him. I stood inside the doorway and looked around. Elyse was already at the table with Jake, and I wasn't about to butt in. Jake was waving at me.

I pretended not to see him.

"Lucky! Hey!" He jogged across the caf and blocked me trying to head to the other side of the room. "Where are you going? I saved you a seat."

"I don't want to intrude," I told him, scanning the room for an empty table.

"Intrude? What are you talking about? Everyone likes you. Come on. Just come sit down."

"Jake," I grabbed his arm, "I don't think Elyse likes me." He frowned.

"Why would you say that?" he asked.

God, boys were so oblivious.

"It's just a feeling I get," I said, rather more sarcastically than I intended.

"She just doesn't know you. Come on. Please?"

"Why do you care?" I asked.

He looked straight into my eyes, and I wondered suddenly if Elyse was watching. I hoped not.

"Because I've been the new kid. I've moved from place to place and wondered if I was just going to get sent away again. It's hard being a foster kid. And I always wished someone had just been nice and invited me to eat with them," he admitted.

"Okay. And thanks," I told him.

"Don't mention it. Come eat before Charlie gets back and accuses me of not taking care of you."

"I don't need anyone to take care of me," I grumbled.

"Lucky, everyone needs someone to look out for them," Jake told me. He sat down, urging everyone to move over a bit to make room at the end for me. There was some good-natured grumbling from the guys at the other end, but Elyse was more vocal with her displeasure.

"There's not enough room," she whined, shifting about half an inch.

"Oh come on, Elyse," Jake slid up against her. "There's plenty of room. See?" He pressed his shoulder up against hers, making her giggle. *Don't roll your eyes, don't roll your eyes!* I told myself. I looked down at my lunch, just to make sure she didn't notice my expression. It was probably to my advantage that Jake paid attention to her and not me.

And just as I had that thought, he turned to me again.

"So, what do you think of Jefferson?" he asked.

"She's good. I was studying *Of Mice and Men* in my old school, but she really gets into it. You know?"

"Yeah. She's fair too. If she sees that you're making an effort, that's what matters to her. She'll really go out of her way to help you."

"That's cool."

"She's also the drama coach. We're putting on *Our Town* this year."

"Really? I love that play!"

"You should try out," he told me.

"I don't think so." I smiled.

"You'd be great. Come on. I'm trying out," he said.

"Are you serious?" I tilted my head and studied his face, trying to decide if he was kidding.

Then Elyse butted in. I had almost managed to forget she was there.

"Jake has played the lead for the past three years."

"Well, not all of them," he said, laughing. "But I've been in all the plays."

"I'm trying out," Elyse informed me, her eyes narrowed.

"See? You should try out too!" Jake said.

I think he completely misread the situation here. I glanced between him and Elyse, then smiled sweetly.

"I don't know how long I'll be here. When my grandmother is feeling better, I'll be able to go home, so probably not a great idea to try out for the play."

"Yeah. I get that." Jake nodded. Elyse seemed pretty happy at the thought of me leaving.

"Too bad," she said, not even looking at me. "It's going to be so much fun. Right, Jake?" She was basically curled into his side like a cat, giving me the side-eye and basically letting me know Jake was hers. I just pasted a smile on my face and ate my lunch.

"So when do you think you'll be going back to your old school, Lucky?" Elyse asked innocently.

"Hopefully soon," I said through teeth that were gritted enough to hurt my jaw. I smiled again.

"Yes, hopefully," she agreed.

Just smile, I told myself. *You'll be out of here before you know it.*

I took out my phone and texted Ryan.

ME:	Red alert. Cheerleader thinks I want her man
RYAN:	Just smile
ME:	Ha. Already smiling

CHAPTER FORTY-ONE
The Audition

"How was lunch?" Charlie caught up to me as I tried to make my escape.

I shrugged.

He frowned at me. "Everything okay?" he asked.

"Yeah. Just…that girl, Elyse. Jake's girlfriend? She hates me."

I expected him to argue. Or defend her. Or reassure me.

I didn't expect him to burst into laughter.

"Why are you laughing?" I asked, frowning.

"Sorry," he gasped between giggles. "I'm not laughing at you. It's just…Elyse hates everyone. Well…she hates any girl she thinks Jake might be interested in. But she's not his girlfriend."

"Does *she* know that?" I asked.

"Yeah. But she hasn't quite accepted it. So she scares off anyone who might be a threat."

"*I'm* not a threat to her!"

"Aren't you? He likes you. I can tell," Charlie said.

"Not like *that!* We're friends," I insisted.

"I'm not the one you need to convince."

I shook my head and sidled past him.

"I'll see you later," I told him. "I can find math class on my own."

"I'll meet you after!" he called to me.

There were mean girls at my old school too. I generally managed to stay under the radar, but the fact that I was thrown together with Jake put me right in the crosshairs. It would be fine. I just had to avoid her until I could get out of here and go home.

I got through math without seeing Elyse.

I made it through English too.

Now all I had to do was get to my locker and meet the guys at the car, and I was home free for another day.

Charlie met me at the door to my English class. Of course. He kept up a steady dialogue all the way to my locker.

"How do you manage to get to all my classes before the bell goes off?" I asked him suddenly.

He blushed.

"I told my teachers I had to help my new foster sister settle in. They said I could help you out for the first week."

"Charlie!" I shoved him playfully. It was kind of sweet. Like having a little brother, I thought for the second time.

Jake was leaning against my locker when we got there. I looked around but thankfully, no Elyse.

"Ready?" I asked, opening my locker and switching out some books.

"Not exactly."

"What do you mean?" I asked distractedly, trying to remember what homework I had to do tonight.

"Tryouts for *Our Town*. They're after school."

"Today? Umm…okay. Is there a bus? Charlie and I can take it. Right, Charlie?"

Charlie looked between me and Jake.

"I'm actually doing the lighting. I always go to the auditions."

"So what am I supposed to do?" I asked, stuffing the last textbook into my bag.

"Come with me. I still think you should try out."

"No way!"

"Then just watch. Please? I could use the moral support." He looked pleadingly at me, hands clasped. "Pleeeease?" He batted his eyelashes at me while he begged.

I smacked him with my bag.

"Fine."

He grinned and took my arm and Charlie's and pulled us toward the theater. I hadn't seen it yet, and I was duly impressed when he pushed the doors open. It was larger than I expected and opulent with red velvet seats and a curtain edged in gold. There were a lot of students trying out; Elyse among them. She was right up front, and I watched as she turned and saw us. Her eyes squinted into slits, but her face cleared up almost instantly as she waved and called out.

"Jake! Over here! I saved you a seat."

"Thanks, Elyse, but I'm going to sit with Charlie and Lucky."

Oh lord. This was bad. So much for staying under the radar.

"Go sit with her," I whispered to him.

"What?"

"Go. Sit. With. Her."

"Why? I'm fine back here." He dropped into a seat and put his feet up on the one in front. Charlie immediately did the same. "Sit down, Lucky."

And what else was I supposed to do? I was already drawing attention. I sat down heavily beside them and tried to ignore the curious glances. And the hostile ones.

One by one, students walked onstage and did monologues. Elyse was one of the first and much as I hated to admit it, she was really good. Much sweeter onstage than she was in real life.

And Jake...Jake blew me away. He was amazing. He actually stopped being Jake and became George. It was incredible.

"He's so good," I breathed to Charlie, smiling.

"I know." He grinned back.

Jake bounded back toward us and stood over me.

"Come on," he said, holding out his hand.

"What? Why?"

"I need a scene partner," he said, reaching down and grabbing my hand, pulling me up. *Oh, hell no.*

"No way! I'm not trying out." I fought against him.

"Lucky, I just need someone to do a scene with. Come on. Please? It'll be fun. You don't have to officially try out. But you said you loved the play, right? Just come up and read with me."

"Is there someone else you can do a scene with? Like Elyse?"

"I don't want to do it with her. Just help me out this once, okay? I'll owe you. I'll do all your chores for a week. A month!"

"Fine. Which scene?"

"Yes!" Jake handed me a script. "This one."

I stood up and followed him.

"I'm supposed to clean the bathrooms, by the way," I told him.

"What? Wait…I didn't agree to bathrooms!"

"Oh, yes you did!"

"Fine. Bathrooms. Just read the scene." He walked up to Ms. Jefferson. "I'll go next. Lucky is going to read with me."

I saw Elyse's mouth drop open.

"Ready?" He was back by my side.

"I guess," I said, not missing the openly hostile group of girls staring at us.

"Then let's go!"

He led me up the stairs and onto the stage. I had been in drama for years and I was no stranger to the stage. But usually the audience didn't hate me before I opened my mouth.

I stood upstage, holding my script lightly, waiting for Jake.

He came up behind me.

"Emily, can I carry your books home for you?"

"Why…thank you. It isn't far."

And just like that, it began. We became Emily and George. And we were good. I forgot everything around me. I forgot about the girls glaring holes through me. I forgot about everything except George and Emily.

We finished the scene and stood staring at each other in the sudden silence of the theater. The silence lasted a moment and then applause. I heard Charlie yell, "Yes!" somewhere beyond the edge of the stage. I saw kids standing out of the corner of my eye. And I saw Ms. Jefferson clapping and smiling broadly.

Jake grinned at me, then grabbed me in a hug.

"That was amazing," he yelled in my ear, lifting me off the ground.

And I was smiling too. And blushing. I admit it. But even as I felt my face grow warm, I pushed it away. I didn't have time for that fluttery feeling Jake was giving me. Not when my grandmother needed me. I ignored it and caught sight of Charlie and smiled wider. I hugged Jake back and over his shoulder saw Elyse staring at me with such hatred that it wiped the smile off my face instantly.

I pulled away from Jake and nodded at him.

"Good job," I said, smacking him on the shoulder like a footballer before walking away from one of the few perfect moments I had experienced in months, the applause still ringing in my ears as I pretended not to see the hurt look on Jake's face.

CHAPTER FORTY-TWO

Confrontation

"Let me just grab my stuff and I'll meet you at the car," I called to Jake and Charlie when we left the theater after the auditions.

"Want me to come with you?" Charlie asked.

"No, I'm good. Be right out."

I dashed toward my locker. I was starving and I had no idea what Sarah was making for dinner, but it was a safe bet it was going to be amazing.

As amazing as the applause had felt.

I was smiling as I grabbed my stuff. I was so distracted, I didn't hear anyone coming up behind me until I was surrounded by a bunch of cheerleaders.

"Running off to see Jake?" one of them asked.

"He's giving me a ride home," I agreed.

"Home?" Another girl laughed.

I ignored that comment.

"You need to leave Jake alone," the first girl said. "He belongs to Elyse."

"He BELONGS to her? Are you serious? So she owns him?"

I really should have kept my mouth shut.

"No, I don't own him. Obviously. But we're together, okay? And I'm not about to let some outsider come in and distract him."

"Look, Elyse. I'm not interested in Jake, okay? You've got nothing to worry about," I told her, closing my locker and looking around me for a way out of this.

"I just don't want you walking around his house in your underwear or something," she said.

Huh?

"It's a foster home, not a brothel. No one is walking around in their underwear. Least of all me. Now if you don't mind, I need to meet Jake and Charlie." I made a move to step around her, and she blocked me. She actually blocked me! "Excuse me," I said calmly, admittedly talking to her like she was a child. "Can I get by?"

"Can I get by?" one of the others mimicked. I pasted a smile on my face. I figured I'd let them have their fun and then get bored and move on.

"Do you really think someone like Jake would be interested in a nasty little slut like you?" Elyse hissed at me.

"Now we know where the term 'get lucky' came from," another girl said, laughing cruelly.

"What did you just say?" I asked, not even knowing who I was talking to at this point.

"Oh, what? Are you going to go all 'war party' on us?" Elyse asked.

"You better shut your mouth," I warned her, my hands clenching into fists.

Elyse grinned suddenly and then started to whoop, doing an awkward version of a war dance around me, patting her hand against her mouth as she went. Within seconds, her friends were following behind.

As Elyse passed me, I turned, and before I could think about what a bad idea it was, I drew my arm back and punched her square in the face. When she didn't go down, I hit her again in the stomach.

She dropped like a stone.

A stone that was gasping for air.

One of the others lunged for me, and I shoved her hard into the lockers. I swung around, ready to hit the next girl to come at me or to run for the door if I could.

And before I could make a break for it, I felt a hand grab my shoulder.

"Lucky!" Ms. Jefferson looked shocked. "What have you done?"

"Me? She started it!"

It was hard to defend myself when Elyse was bleeding on the floor.

"I don't care who started it. Elyse, we'd better call your parents. Lucky, just come with me."

The girls had helped Elyse up and were supporting her as she walked.

"What do you expect from someone like her? She's trash," Elyse sniffed.

"Indian trash," someone else said.

I looked over at Ms. Jefferson, who had to have heard, but she was looking straight ahead.

CHAPTER FORTY-THREE
Unexpected Kindness

I waited outside the principal's office for what felt like an hour. They had called Sarah and Edward, and I felt terrible. They were so nice, and I knew this would disappoint them. I didn't start the fight but somehow, I didn't think that would matter.

I was touching a sore spot on my head where it had hit a locker and where a bump was steadily rising when Sarah walked into the office. She sat down heavily beside me.

"Are you all right?" she asked. I almost burst into tears at her unexpected kindness. I nodded, swallowing the lump in my throat. "The principal said they were going to expel you. Do you want to tell me what happened?"

I wasn't even sure I could speak. I had been expecting to be kicked out again, but she was being so nice to me. I didn't deserve it. My grandparents would be ashamed of how I had acted. I knew that. They had taught me to be better than the people who treated us badly. But I had never had much patience for racist pieces of garbage like Elyse.

"She called me trash and started doing a war dance around me." I sniffled, wiping angrily at my eyes.

"She *what?*" Now Sarah looked like she wanted to punch someone. "Did you tell anyone?"

"Who's going to believe me?" I asked.

"I do! Stay here. I'm going to have a word with the principal."

Sarah stormed off, leaving me alone. Almost. Charlie poked his head around the corner about five seconds later.

"The coast is clear," he whispered over his shoulder. He sidled in like a secret agent with Jake right behind him. "She told us to wait in the car," Charlie said, falling into the chair beside me. Jake sat on my other side.

"Are you okay?" he asked. I nodded. "What happened? All we heard was that there was a fight and you were being kicked out for punching Elyse."

"She's a racist little bitch and she started it," I blurted out. "She called me trash. NO! She called me *Indian* trash. And she did a war dance."

"Are you serious?" Jake asked. Charlie looked unsurprised. I nodded.

"I'm sorry, Lucky. Is Sarah talking to the principal?" he asked. I nodded. "Well, she can probably talk them out of expelling you. Especially if you told her what Elyse said."

"I did. But I don't know. She said it right in front of Ms. Jefferson, and she didn't say anything."

Jake put an arm around me, squeezing wordlessly, while Charlie hugged me violently from the other side. I was tearing up again. They didn't even know me, but they were being as fiercely protective as I'd expect Ryan to be in the same situation.

Sarah reappeared then, stopping suddenly in front of us.

"I thought you guys were going to wait in the car," she said.

"Lucky needed us," Charlie said.

"Am I being expelled?" I asked. Sarah smiled suddenly.

"No. I told him if he was going to expel you and not the other girls, I'd go to the school board and complain. He agreed to give you another chance. But Lucky…you can't get into fights. It's not something Edward and I are willing to put up with. Understand?"

I nodded, extricating myself from the boys and standing up.

"I do. Thank you for talking to him for me."

She tilted her head to the side and studied me.

"Of course. As long as you're staying with us, we're your family, Lucky. And we've got your back. Right boys?"

"Right!" Charlie yelled. Jake nodded.

"Yeah. We do," he said, leading the way out and back home.

CHAPTER FORTY-FOUR

Flying Under the Radar

My life continued with me basically spending my days trying to avoid Elyse. I had my lunch switched so I no longer saw Jake, but Charlie kept me company. And we didn't have any classes together anyway, so as long as I took the long way to most of my classes and avoided the hall where her locker was, I pretty much managed to fly under the radar.

After my "violent outburst," I didn't make the cast of the play. I tried not to care. I pretended I didn't. But being up onstage with Jake had been amazing, and I wished I could be up there rehearsing and having fun with the rest of the cast. Elyse had got the part instead, so I helped paint sets in the art room on the other side of the school, well away from the theater.

"How are they doing?" I asked Charlie, who met me outside just before the cast left the theater so I could stay out of

Elyse's way. It seemed ridiculous that *I* was the one who had to go out of my way to avoid *her*. But I was also the one who had something to lose, so I kept far away and jealously wished it was me on the stage.

"Good. Jake is amazing. But Elyse can't remember her lines. And she overacts. It's annoying."

I laughed.

"Are you saying that just to make me feel better?" I asked, leaning against the car and shoving him with my shoulder.

"No! I'm serious. She sucks. She's as awful an actress as she is a person." He grinned.

I laughed again.

"Well, isn't this cozy?" said a voice that sounded so close to the Wicked Witch of the West that it sent a shiver down my spine. I had always hated that character. My own personal wicked witch was sauntering up with her band of flying monkeys. "And I thought you were after your older foster brother. I didn't realize you liked younger men," she cackled.

Charlie stood up, squaring his shoulders, and opened his mouth to respond. I stepped in front of him, pushing him back gently against the car.

"Hi, Elyse. I hear you're killing it in rehearsals," I said, smiling in what I thought was a friendly way, but my facial expression felt suspiciously like a grimace.

"Aren't you sweet," she cooed. "Jake and I have pretty amazing chemistry onstage. And off, if you know what I mean." She threw her head back and laughed kind of maniacally, I thought.

Charlie was struggling to get around me.

"Don't start anything," I muttered, putting myself firmly between him and Elyse again.

"I'm not starting anything," Elyse said, frowning.

"I wasn't talking to you. We're good, right?" I nodded her way, then glanced back at Charlie who was glaring at Elyse. "Right, Charlie?"

"Aww. Look at her protecting her little man. Lucky is all boo'd up with someone on her own level this time."

"What are you talking about?" I asked. She was exhausting, and I had my hands full with Charlie. Where the hell was Jake?

"Well you never had a chance in hell with Jake. But look at you. You got yourself a little Mexican boy to play with. Birds of a feather, right?"

"I'm Dominican!" Charlie yelled, trying to push past me. I had dropped my bag and was literally holding him back.

"Charlie, stop!" He was stronger than he looked, and I was grunting with the effort of holding onto him.

"Dominican, Mexican. Who cares? They're both brown. Why don't you just go back to wherever it is that you came from?"

What did she just say? I nearly lost my grip on Charlie for a second and fought to hang on to him. I pulled on the back of his jacket. He was yelling at her in Spanish now.

"Calm down, kid. Even you can do better than this Indian whore." She spit at me, and I felt bits of it hit my face. I was so shocked, I lost my grip on Charlie, who stumbled. I wiped saliva off my face and stared at her. She walked toward me, sneering. "You're a piece of shit, Lucky. No one wants your worthless ass. That's why you're in foster care. Not Jake. Not even the little Mexican here. No one will ever want you." She was right in front of me now. "You're nothing. An Indian whore who has nothing to offer except what's between your legs."

I heard Charlie yell "Soy Dominicano!" as I pulled my arm back, my hand clenched tightly. But I didn't see him until I felt my fist connect solidly with the person in front of me. The person who, a second ago, had been Elyse. But Charlie had somehow ducked away and gotten between us, and my fist hit him in the side of the head so hard, he went down, his face bouncing off the pavement. I heard a scream and only vaguely recognized it as my own as I pushed someone out of the way and fell to the ground beside him.

"CHARLIE!" I screamed. He was limp, his eyes closed, with blood dripping down his face. "CALL 911!" I shrieked, watching as Elyse and her friends turned and walked away without raising their phones.

"I hope she killed him," I heard Elyse say as I cradled Charlie's head in my lap.

"Help!" I yelled, whipping my head from side to side, trying to see where my bag was so I could grab my phone.

"Lucky?" It was Jake. He was here and he'd help.

"Jake, please. Call 911. Charlie…he's unconscious. Oh my god. I think I killed him." I was hysterical. Jake knelt down beside me, pulling his phone out of his pocket and touching Charlie's face.

"He's not dead, Lucky. Calm down. Yes. I'm at Weston Heights High. Can you send an ambulance? My friend is unconscious. I don't know what happened. Yes, he's breathing. Okay. Thank you." He hung up just as Charlie started to move, groaning.

"Oh my god! Charlie! Stay still. You're hurt."

"Lucky, what the hell happened?" He was dialing again. "Sarah? It's me. Charlie got hurt. The ambulance is on its way, but can you meet us at the hospital? I don't know. Okay."

"I...we were talking and Elyse came out and called him Mexican and said she thought he should go back to where he came from and he was upset and then she called me worthless and a slut...and she spit at me. I lost my temper. I tried to hit her but Charlie got in the way." I was sobbing even though Charlie was now struggling to sit up.

"Stay down, man." Jake held him down gently. "You're all right, Charlie, but you need a doctor." He looked over at me. "You knocked him out?"

"No! I don't think so. I hit him by mistake and he went down and hit his head on the ground. I think that knocked him out. Oh my god, Charlie. I'm so sorry."

"Stop crying on me, Lucky!" he croaked.

The ambulance arrived then, and EMTs pulled me away and strapped Charlie to a stretcher.

"Do I have to go to school tomorrow?" he asked one of the EMTs.

"Probably not," the guy said, laughing. He shone a light in Charlie's eyes. "I think you have a concussion."

"Is he okay?" I asked him desperately. "Did I give him brain damage?"

"I doubt it. He seems fine, but we'll take him in and have him checked out. You can meet us there."

Jake pulled me away so the EMTs could get Charlie in the ambulance.

"Come on. We'll follow in the car."

I got in. Numb at first. Then scared. Terrified that Charlie would lapse into a coma or something before we got there. Or that he'd have some kind of lasting brain damage that changed him entirely. Or that he'd be dead.

"Can you go faster?" I begged Jake. He stepped down on the pedal and we lurched forward. Sarah was getting out of her car when we pulled up.

"What happened?" she asked, looking terrified. "Where is he?" Jake took her arm and started leading her to the front of the hospital.

"The ambulance brought him in. He's awake. I think he's okay. Maybe just a concussion. But they need to check him out."

"A concussion! What happened to him?"

We were at the door now. I opened my mouth to answer. Then closed it.

"Lucky?" She stopped and turned to me. She was even more scared than I was. She loved him. I could see it all over her face. I was about to answer…or try to, when Edward ran up.

"Where is he? Is he okay?" He looked frantic, and I realized all over again how much these two loved the boys. Maybe could have loved me. "What happened?" He was looking at Jake.

"It was me," I told them, stepping in front of Jake. "It's my fault."

"You did this?" Edward asked incredulously. I nodded. "How?"

"I...I was aiming for Elyse, and Charlie got in the way. I hit him by mistake and he...he hit the ground hard. With his head," I clarified.

"Oh my god." Edward turned and bolted through the doorway, closely followed by Sarah.

"Come on," Jake said, holding out his hand. I hesitated for a second. But I couldn't put off seeing Charlie forever. If I had hurt him in some way that was going to affect him for the rest of his life, I needed to know. I needed to see for myself if he was all right. I took Jake's hand and let him lead me in after Sarah and Edward.

"I didn't mean to hurt him," I whispered.

"I know you didn't. He'll be fine, Lucky."

"How do you know?" I asked.

"I don't. But let's go find out."

I nodded, following, trying not to look at all the people in various stages of injury or illness lining the hallways.

"He's in here," Sarah called, leading us through a set of double doors and into a hallway that was alive with doctors and nurses, machines beeping, and a few patients wheeling machines looped with tubes and wires around beside them.

Charlie seemed so small tucked into his bed. A doctor

and nurse were talking quietly while the nurse made notes on a clipboard. Charlie looked pale and sickly with his head sporting a bandage and his eyes closed. The doctor looked up.

"Are you the family?" he asked. Edward and Sarah nodded, clinging to each other. "He's asleep. We have to wake him up hourly because he has a concussion. He took quite a knock to the head."

I stared at Charlie while the doctor spoke, willing him to be okay, to wake up. To be his happy, puppy-dog self again. But he slept on, with just the odd movement of his eyelids and the beeping of a heart monitor to show he was still alive.

"Is he going to be okay?" I choked out.

The doctor glanced at me.

"Yes. He'll be fine. He'll have a massive headache for a day or two, but he'll be back to normal before you know it."

"Oh, thank god!" Sarah said, lowering herself into a chair beside the bed and taking Charlie's hand in hers. Edward stood behind her, his hands on her shoulders.

"You should go home," he told Jake. "Both of you. Get some sleep."

"Okay. Tell him we were here, when he wakes up," Jake said, pulling me toward the door. I wanted to stay. I wanted to be there when he woke up so I could tell him how sorry I was. That it had been an accident. That I would do anything to take it back.

CHAPTER FORTY-FIVE
Another Morning

I didn't sleep much that night. I'd drift off and then wake up suddenly, remembering the sound Charlie's head had made when it hit the ground. Like a melon. Or a pumpkin. And I'd feel sick to my stomach until I convinced myself over and over again that he'd be okay. I got up the next morning before the sun rose. Sarah and Edward hadn't come back from the hospital, and the house was deadly silent. I sipped a cup of Earl Grey and watched the sky change color.

Jake wandered into the kitchen at virtually the same moment that Sarah and Edward walked in. All three looked exhausted.

"How is he?" Jake asked before I even had a chance to open my mouth.

"Yeah," I blurted out. "Is he all right?"

Sarah nodded. She looked tired.

"The doctor said he'll be fine. They're keeping him until later today to run a couple more tests. Just to be sure," she said, seeing Jake and me open our mouths to ask.

"But the thing is…" Edward said, glancing over at Sarah. "He just as easily could have been *not* okay. You could have… it could have been *a lot* worse, Lucky."

"I know," I said, my eyes filling up again, despite my claim that I never cried. "And I'm so sorry. I didn't mean to hurt him."

"But you meant to hurt someone else," Sarah said. "The school called and told us you were fighting with that girl again." She shook her head. She was sorry. I could see that. I had hurt Sarah and Edward just as much as I had hurt Charlie. Maybe more.

"They're expelling you," Edward said. "We're sorry, Lucky. But Cynthia is coming to pick you up."

"You're sending her away?" Jake asked. "It wasn't even her fault. Elyse spit at her! She called both of them names."

"The school won't reconsider. I called and tried to talk them out of it." Sarah looked at me regretfully. "It's your second fight, and you were on probation for the first one. And you seriously hurt Charlie…I know it was an accident." She held her hands up before I could argue. "I believe you, Lucky. But if you can't go back to school…it's the only high school in our district. You have to be moved to a home in another district."

"I could bus to another school!" I pled, looking from Sarah to Edward. "Please! I like it here! Don't make me leave." I was openly crying now. Jake put an arm around me, looking at Sarah and Edward.

"Can she do that? Just go to another school? I'll go with her," he said.

"It doesn't work that way. I'm sorry. We both are," Sarah said. She was crying too now. She pulled me away from Jake and into a hug.

The doorbell rang.

Cynthia from Children's Aid was on the other side. She smiled, but her smile looked forced.

"You better go pack, Lucky," she said.

I went upstairs, pulling my things out of drawers and off hangers and stuffing all of it back into my bag. I took the photos from the night table and stared at Grandma and Grandpa before adding them to my things. Lastly, I took my phone and texted Ryan.

ME: I got into a fight
RYAN: Again?
ME: Yeah. Same girl
RYAN: Did you win?
ME: Not funny.
RYAN: It kind of is. RU OK?
ME: No. I hurt one of my foster brothers. I have to leave
RYAN: The school?
ME: And the house
RYAN: RU serious?

ME:	Yah
RYAN:	Where RU going?
ME:	I don't know yet
RYAN:	If u don't stay in one place, I'll never get to visit!
ME:	I know. I'm sorry. Want to meet me at Grandma's sometime?
RYAN:	Sure!
ME:	Kk
RYAN:	So what happened?
ME:	I got spit on by the cheerleader who did the war dance. She called me and Charlie names
RYAN:	I hope you knocked her on her ass
ME:	I tried
RYAN:	Good
ME:	Not good. I hit Charlie by mistake
RYAN:	You never could hit what you were aiming for...
ME:	I messed up big time. Charlie is in the hospital
RYAN:	WHAT? Is he ok?
ME:	He will be. But I'm expelled. I have to move to a home in another district
RYAN:	Shit. Sorry Lucky
ME:	Thx
RYAN:	Text me when you get there
ME:	Kk

CHAPTER FORTY-SIX

Cynthia from Children's Aid

I still hadn't made it back to the house to get some stuff for my grandmother.

I still hadn't managed to see Ryan.

And I still hadn't visited Grandma for a few days. I needed to call her.

But the bigger issue was Cynthia, who was trying to find me a place to stay. She stopped at a coffee shop and made some calls while I sipped a hot chocolate.

"No. She needs a place tonight. Right. Are you sure? Okay, thanks anyway."

This wasn't her first call.

"No luck?" I asked. She frowned at me but didn't answer.

"Hi, is this Kevin? Hi Kevin. It's Cynthia from Children's Aid."

I tuned her out. Honestly, if she didn't find a place soon,

I was going to suggest I stay with Ryan again. I know "it wasn't an option" before, but it had to be better than sleeping on the streets.

Or in Cynthia's Prius.

"Okay. Thanks."

"You found a place?" I asked.

"No. Drink your hot chocolate."

"Hi, is this Paula? Hi Paula, it's Cynthia from Children's Aid."

ME:	CfromCA can't find a place for me
RYAN:	Stay here
ME:	Right? If she doesn't find a place, I'm so there
RYAN:	Sorry this is happening to you
ME:	It's fine. Once Grandma is better, I'll be home
RYAN:	Lucky...

I watched the dots blinking for a minute then gave up.

ME:	What???
RYAN:	She might not get better. At least not better enough to come home
ME:	She will
RYAN:	...
ME:	SHE WILL
RYAN:	Ok
ME:	I'll let u know where I am. If she ever finds a place

"I found a place!" Cynthia looked triumphant.

"Oh goody," I muttered.

"I think you'll be happy with this one," she said.

"Oh, yeah. It's just awesome being sent to a new place every other week. And none of them are home!"

"This one was your own fault, Lucky. Let's not forget that. You're going to end up in juvenile detention if you're not careful!"

"Are you serious? I haven't committed a crime!" I shouted.

"You did, actually! You assaulted another girl! And you could have really hurt Charlie!"

"She started it!" I insisted. "And I didn't mean to hit Charlie."

Cynthia took a deep breath and then started again.

"Listen. I know this isn't easy. I know things are beyond your control, and your first home wasn't a good fit."

"You mean the 'home' where the foster father tried to sexually assault me?"

Cynthia clenched her jaw before continuing.

"I found you a place you can go to tonight, and it's close enough that you can attend your old school."

"Wait…the one I was at today?"

"No, Lucky. They expelled you. Remember? I mean the school you went to when you lived with your grandmother."

"Are you serious?" I asked, barely daring to breath in case she took it all back.

"Yes."

"Oh my god…thank you!"

"I'd say 'no problem,' but it was a huge problem. Just… try not to get yourself kicked out of this one."

"I will," I promised her.

ME: I GET TO COME BACK TO SCHOOL!

RYAN: Srsly?

ME: Yes! I'll see you tomorrow!

RYAN: YAY!

CHAPTER FORTY-SEVEN

Home #3

It's not really surprising that my eyes were focused somewhere around my height when the door to the latest in my ever-growing list of foster homes opened. But I was about three feet too high.

"Hi!" a tiny little person chirped at me.

I adjusted my gaze and saw a kid who should be starring in a Disney movie. She was literally that cute.

"Hi." I grinned at her. It was hard not to smile at her impish little face with her front teeth missing. She had pigtails. Actual pigtails.

"Is Paula home?" Cynthia from Children's Aid asked.

"PAULA!" the girl yelled without taking her eyes off me. I laughed.

"What's your name?" I asked her.

"Lucy."

"No way! We have almost the same name! I'm Lucky." I stuck out my hand and she shook it.

"Your name's Lucky?" She giggled.

"Swear to God," I told her solemnly.

"That's so funny!"

A woman came to the door then.

"Lucy, can you help Greg with the dishes, please?"

As Lucy skipped away, the woman smiled at me, pushing the hair out of her face and basically looking like she badly needed a day off.

"You must be Lucky?"

I nodded.

"Well, you're welcome here, Lucky. My husband is just doing the dishes, and you've already met Lucy."

"Okay. Thanks for having me?" I wasn't sure what to say, but she smiled and held the door open for me.

"Thanks, Cynthia. I'll give you a shout tomorrow after Lucky is settled."

"Thank you, Paula. You're a life saver!" Paula closed the door with a wave.

"Case workers are so dramatic," she said, rolling her eyes at me. I smiled back. "Come on. I'll introduce you to Greg."

Greg turned out to resemble pretty much what I pictured a lumberjack to look like. He was tall and broad-shouldered with hair that looked like it took a lot of effort to tame. But his smile was warm, and he shook my hand gently.

"It's nice to meet you, Lucky. We're glad to have you. Right, Lucy?" He grabbed a handful of bubbles out of the sink and blew them at Lucy. She shrieked and smacked him with her dish towel.

"Come on, Lucky. I'll show you your room," Paula said.

"I'll show her! Please?" Lucy gave Paula her winning smile.

"If it's okay with Lucky," Paula told her, smoothing her hair back.

"Can I?" Lucy implored. How could I say no?

"Of course." I smiled. Which is how I found myself following a bounding pig-tailed kid up the stairs and into a room that looked more or less exactly like the last two. Except this one had twin beds.

"Do we share a room?" I asked her.

"No!" She collapsed onto one of the beds in a fit of giggles. "My room is next door."

"Cool!" I dropped my bag on the floor and pulled out my photos, setting them carefully on the night table.

"Who are they?" Lucy asked, leaning over to study each of them. She gently touched the one of Grandma, Grandpa, and me.

"My grandparents. And me, obviously."

"Where are they?"

"My grandfather died and my grandmother...is in a home. She has Alzheimer's...trouble remembering things." My eyes prickled. I had never said that out loud.

"I'm sorry," Lucy said, slipping her hand into mine.

I squeezed it. "Thanks."

She rolled onto her back and studied me.

"Do you miss them?" she asked.

"Every single day," I admitted.

She nodded.

"I miss my mom a lot. I lived with her. Before, I mean."

"Is she…?"

Lucy looked away, her face coloring.

"She's in jail."

"Oh." I had no idea how to respond to that.

"We didn't have any money so she stole some stuff. She told me it was wrong and to never steal. But we were hungry. She'll be out soon though. Just in time for her birthday." She smiled a little.

"That's good. And I'm really sorry that your mom got…" Caught? I didn't even know what I was sorry for. "That your mom got sent away." She nodded.

"Do you want to see my room?" she asked suddenly, jumping up.

"For sure!" I said, happy to change the subject.

CHAPTER FORTY-EIGHT
Good Night

By the time Lucy had shown me my room and then wandered off to hers, I could barely keep my eyes open. It had been a long day. I was exhausted from moving again. I was excited to see Ryan tomorrow. And I wanted nothing more than to climb into bed and put this day behind me. But as I got under the blankets, I knew I had to do one more thing if I had any hope of sleeping tonight.

ME: Hey. It's Lucky.

...

...

...

I was about to give up and just turn my phone off for the night when I finally got a response.

JAKE: Hey. U ok?
ME: Yeah. How's Charlie?
JAKE: Fine. Bit of a headache but cracking jokes again. He liked the comics you left him
ME: I wish I could have said good-bye
JAKE: He knows. It's okay
ME: I'm sorry.
JAKE: I know.

I paused, trying to figure out what to say, then just took a breath and typed.

ME: Maybe I can visit?

I waited, my hands shaking a little.

JAKE: You better!

Smiling, I said good night and tossed my phone onto the night table before turning off the light.

CHAPTER FORTY-NINE
Old Friends

I woke up early. Something that rarely happened on a school day. Like most teens, I usually had to drag myself out of bed and force myself to go to school.

But not today.

Today I was going back to *my* school!

I got dressed quickly, hoping I might get the chance to pick up some of my clothes soon since I was close to home. I was down the stairs before I could really take a good look at my Beatles T-shirt and jeans.

"Good morning," I sang out, sitting down at the table and picking up a piece of toast.

"Peanut butter?" Lucy asked.

"My name's Lucky, but I'd love some peanut butter," I quipped. She laughed.

"Can I get you anything else?" Paula asked.

"No thanks. Cynthia said I could just walk to school?" I asked, standing back up.

"Yes. But I can drive you if you'd like."

"No. I'm fine. Does Lucy walk too?" I asked. Truthfully, I didn't want to wait. I was dying to see Ryan and everyone else.

"No. I take her."

"Okay. Well…have a great day!" I headed for the door before remembering. "Oh! I was hoping to drop by my house… where I lived before…to grab a few things. Is that okay?"

"Just be back for dinner," Paula said.

"I will. Bye, Lucy."

She waved, her mouth full of something I couldn't identify.

I couldn't stop looking around as I walked to school. Ryan had offered to pick me up, but he had the school paper in the morning and had to be there early, so I declined. I was coming from the opposite direction of my house, but I knew the neighborhood, and after being away I couldn't stop staring at everything that was familiar.

The walk was over far too soon, and I was climbing the front stairs of my old school before I knew it. Kids I had known most of my life were watching me walk up.

"Hey, Lucky!" one of the drama kids called out. "Are you back?"

"Yes!"

I barely knew her but she ran over and hugged me. I hugged her back. I was finally home!

"Hi, Lucky!" someone else called out. Taylor. I did know her and rushed over to give her a hug.

"Hi!" I was still hugging Taylor when I heard a shout from the parking lot.

"LUCKY!"

I turned and saw Ryan running toward me like a linebacker.

"OhmygodRYAN!" I shrieked and, dropping my bag, ran for him. We collided somewhere in the middle, and he wrapped his arms around me and flung me off my feet. I was literally crying. And I never cried. But suddenly, after all the stuff I had been through, having Ryan right in front of me was just so incredibly overwhelming.

"Are you crying?" he asked, trying to pull away. I clung to him like a spider monkey.

"No!" I insisted, wiping my eyes on his shoulder.

"Oh my god! Lucky Robinson is actually crying!" he crowed. "You never cry."

"I'm not crying!" I squeezed the breath out of him. "I missed you so much!" I told him.

"I missed you too." I looked over his shoulder and grinned.

"Hi, Thomas," I called out.

"Hi, Lucky. Welcome back. Sorry…I didn't want to intrude."

"You're not." I finally let go of Ryan to give Thomas a quick hug. "So are you guys…official?"

"You know I don't subscribe to labels, Lucky." Ryan grinned.

"Ignore him. The answer is yes," Thomas said, taking Ryan's hand and kissing him on the cheek.

"Aww. You're adorable."

"Please shut up." Ryan smiled happily.

"I don't know if you guys have plans, but I want to drop by my house after school to pick some stuff up for Grandma."

"Thomas has basketball, but I can take you. Just...please tell me you're going to pick up some clothes too?"

"Whatever do you mean?" I asked innocently.

"I *mean*...what look are you going for here?" he asked, gesturing toward my jeans and T-shirt.

"You bought me this shirt." I laughed.

"Well, I do have impeccable taste," he admitted.

"Come on. I have to drop by the office so I can get my schedule."

We walked into the school like I hadn't left. If I could manage to stay out of trouble, my life would almost be back to normal. I'd be going to my old school with my friends, right near my house. At least until Grandma came home. I vowed right there in the foyer of the school that I would not cause any trouble this time. Or let anyone cause trouble for me.

CHAPTER FIFTY
Grandma's Stuff

The day flew by. People stopped me in the halls to say hi and welcome me back. Ryan was by my side as much as he possibly could be. And the teachers all seemed pretty happy to have me back. It was a homecoming, and it felt amazing.

Thomas beat me to Ryan's locker after the last bell, and I hung back and (in a non-creepy way) watched them. I loved seeing my best friend so happy. Thomas said something, making Ryan laugh and lean into him affectionately. He had changed since I had last been here. He was more confident and comfortable being himself. I loved Thomas suddenly for that.

"You two are disgustingly adorable," I said, walking up and leaning against the lockers beside me.

"I know," Ryan said happily, giving Thomas a quick kiss before sending him to basketball practice.

"See you tomorrow, Lucky," Thomas called over his shoulder.

"You bet!" I looked at Ryan, who was staring after his boyfriend. I shoved him. "Snap out of it, Romeo. Are you ready to go?"

"Yeah." He had the kind of smile on his face that was impossible to wipe off.

"You look happy," I told him. "It looks good on you."

"Yeah, he's pretty great," he agreed. "How's your grandma doing?"

"I haven't seen her for a while. And the last time I did, she wasn't herself," I admitted.

"That's rough."

"Yeah. I should call her and see what she wants me to bring from the house."

I whipped out my phone and found her number.

"Hello?" Her voice sounded much stronger than the last time I had spoken to her.

"Hi, Grandma. It's Lucky."

"Lucky girl! How are you, sweetheart?" Wow. She sounded like her old self again!

"I'm good, Grandma. I'm back at my old school, and Ryan is going to take me to the house to pick some things up for you. Is there anything you want me to bring you?"

"Oreos?" she asked hopefully.

"I'll bring you Oreos, Grandma. But what do you want from the house?"

"Oh, dear. Can you bring my cookie jar?"

"For the Oreos?"

"Obviously, dear. And my blue cardigan. And my slippers. And the book I was reading. And maybe some photos?"

"I'll find all of that."

"When are you coming?" she asked.

"I'm not sure. Maybe tomorrow?"

"All right, dear. Just call first, okay? I have a poker tournament scheduled."

"Oh. Okay. Bye, Grandma. Love you. Ryan says hi."

"Bye, sweetheart. Love you both."

"She says she loves you too," I told Ryan.

"Awww. Are you ready now?"

"Yeah, let's go."

I couldn't stop staring out the window on the drive to my house.

"You look like a golden retriever," Ryan said, laughing.

"I forgot how amazing my neighborhood is," I told him.

"What do you mean?"

"All the places I've stayed are so generic. All the streets are the same. The houses are the same. My room is always the same. But this? Look at all the houses. They're all different. I miss this," I sighed.

"You're so weird."

"I know. Look—there's my house! I missed you so much, house!"

I was out the door and dashing up the front steps before Ryan had brought the car to a full stop. I slid my key into the lock and threw the front door open.

"I'm home!" I yelled out to the empty house, the smell of smoke still heavy in the air.

I walked through the living room, running my hands over my grandfather's chair, picturing him sitting there reading while Grandma puttered around in the kitchen. I looked toward it but decided to avoid going into the room where this whole mess started.

"Lucky?" Ryan called out from the doorway.

"In here."

"Wow. It's like you never left," he said, looking around.

"Except for the smell of smoke," I reminded him.

We went upstairs and into my grandparents' bedroom. Even after all this time, I could still smell the intertwined scents of his cologne and her perfume mingling with the smoky air, and I missed them both so terribly much in that moment that I wasn't sure I could stand it. But with a deep breath, I opened the closet and pulled out Grandma's cardigan.

"Is her book on the nightstand?" I asked Ryan.

"This one?" he held up a Stephen King novel.

"Yep. She loves Stephen King." I grinned. "Wow. I really miss being home."

"I know," Ryan said, coming around the bed to hug me. "What else do you need?"

"Could you go into the kitchen and get her cookie jar?"

"Sure."

He left me alone in the room while I found Grandma's slippers and a few other things. I lingered over the photos she had framed on her dresser. I picked up her wedding photo and a picture of the three of us and added them to the pile, then went back for a picture of me holding up a fish with a toothless grin on my face.

I wandered to my room and stood right in the middle, looking around. It was the polar opposite of every room I had been forced to stay in since Cynthia from Children's Aid decided to ruin my life. The walls were a soft buttery yellow and covered in photos I had taken and pictures I had drawn. I took a photo of me and Ryan off the wall and then opened my closet. I badly needed some clothes, but given that I didn't stay in any one house for more than a couple of weeks, my stuff had to fit into one bag. I took out a couple of outfits and folded them as small as I could. I figured I could fit maybe two more outfits and an extra T-shirt. I didn't know how to condense my life into a backpack.

"Are you ready?" Ryan asked, walking in with the cookie jar. He held it up. "It was kind of dirty, so I washed it."

"Yeah, thanks."

"Want me to drop you off at…well, I was going to say home, but…this is home. So…your foster house?"

"Yes, please. Thanks for doing this," I said.

"You know I'd do anything for you, Lucky," he said, giving me a one-armed hug.

CHAPTER FIFTY-ONE

Lucy

Ryan came in to introduce himself and say hi to everyone. As usual, he charmed them and accepted their invitation to stay for dinner. Lucy, of course, loved him.

"Are you gay?" she asked.

"Lucy! Why would you ask that?" Paula said.

"Because the wallpaper on his phone is him and another boy."

"It's okay," Ryan assured her. "Yes, I am. That's my boyfriend."

"Cool," Lucy said. "My teacher is gay. He doesn't have a boyfriend though."

"How would you know that?" Greg laughed.

"He told us when we talked about different kinds of families. It's okay to be gay, you know," she told him, spearing a carrot and nibbling on the end.

"Yes, I know," Greg told her.

"We don't judge people," Lucy announced.

"No, we don't," Paula agreed.

"Okay then. What's your boyfriend's name, Ryan?"

"Thomas," he said, grinning.

"I like that name. Do you want to see my room later?"

"Sure."

She grabbed him as soon as she finished eating and dragged him away.

"I'd be happy to clear the table by myself, guys. Thanks!"

"I'm glad you're close to your friends again, Lucky," Paula said.

"Yeah. It's pretty great. By the way, I have to drop my Grandma's stuff off tomorrow. Is that okay?"

"As long as you get your homework done."

"I will."

The evening flew by. Lucy hung out with Ryan and me until Greg made her come and watch TV with him to give us a break. I hugged Ryan, holding him close, and reminded him I'd see him tomorrow.

I got ready for bed and was crawling under the blankets by about ten o'clock. It was quiet enough that I could hear the soft drone of the television downstairs and a muffled noise from the other side of the wall. I pressed my ear against it and listened. Lucy was crying.

I got up and went to her room and knocked softly on her door.

"Yes?" a muffled voice answered.

"Lucy?" I poked my head in. "Are you okay?"

The streetlight streaming through her window showed the saddest face I had ever seen, and it was streaked with tears. I went and sat down beside her, putting an arm around her shoulders. She wrapped her arms around me tightly, sobbing.

"What's wrong?" I asked gently.

"I miss my mom," she cried.

"Oh Lucy. I'm sorry. I wish I could help. Maybe you could write her a letter."

She nodded.

"Don't you miss your mom?" she sniffled.

"No," I admitted. "My mom isn't very nice. But I miss my grandma."

"And your grandpa too?" she asked, wiping her face on her sleeve.

"Yes. Him especially."

"Can you help me make a present for my mom? Her birthday is coming."

"Of course. I bet she'll be really happy you remembered." I tucked her back in and stood up to leave.

"Lucky?"

"Yeah?"

"Can I sleep in your room tonight?"

"Sure." I held my hand out, and she jumped up to grab it, turning quickly to retrieve a stuffed dog.

"My mom gave him to me," she said, holding him against her chest. "His name is Walter."

"He looks like a Walter," I told her, leading her next door to my room.

I tucked her into the twin bed across from mine.

"Okay now?" I asked.

"Yes."

I got into my own bed and pulled up the blankets.

"Lucky?"

"Yeah?"

"Thanks."

"Anytime," I told her, and meant it. Being away from home was hard enough as a teen. I couldn't even imagine what it must be like for Lucy.

CHAPTER FIFTY-TWO
Grandma

For once, I managed to get into the city to visit Grandma without transferring buses a million times. Ryan offered to take me, and I eagerly took him up on it. With a mochaccino and a donut in hand, the drive to Sunset took half the time. I glanced into the carrier bag at my feet.

"Do you think I forgot anything?" I asked Ryan.

"Aside from packing her furniture, I think you got pretty much everything you could bring," he said.

"Funny."

"I am, aren't I?"

"Oh, you're hilarious. Grandma is definitely going to be happy to see you," I told him.

"I miss her. And your grandfather."

"Me too," I told him. "Do you think Grandma will be… okay today?" I asked him. I wanted her to be herself again. I wanted Ryan to see her the way she used to be and not who she was the last time I saw her.

I wondered if she was ever going to be the same. I wondered if she was going to become less and less herself. I wondered if she was ever going to be able to go home again. Ryan had told me she wasn't going to get better. And since the last time I saw her, I had been wondering if he was right. At the same time, I was afraid to admit that he might be.

And if she couldn't go home, that meant I couldn't either.

"We're here," Ryan nodded toward the Sunset building.

"Right."

He pulled into a parking spot right out front, and I led the way into the building.

"Holy cow!" he breathed. "This place is amazing! Think they'd let us move in?"

"Her room is pretty big. We can probably put a bunk bed in there. Did I tell you they have a spa?"

"Are you serious?"

"Yeah. Grandma can get her hair done without even leaving home."

"That's it. I'm moving in."

I laughed and signed us in. "Her room is down this hall."

Ryan followed me, gawking around as we went. "Honestly, Lucky…this place is really nice. Your grandma is lucky to be here."

"I know," I admitted, knocking on her door.

We both jumped back as Grandma flung it open like she'd been waiting on the other side.

"Hi!" She hugged me tightly and then turned to Ryan and pulled him into a hug too. "It's so lovely to see you both. Come on in."

She ushered us inside. Her room was less sterile than it had been the last time I visited. It was more homey. More like Grandma. She was settling in, and it scared the hell out of me.

"Wow. This is really nice," Ryan told her, looking around.

"Thank you. What did you bring me?" she asked. I handed her the bag, and she started pulling things out. "Oh, this is wonderful. Thank you!" She placed her photographs carefully on her dresser, then dug back into the bag, pulling out each item I had brought for her. As she put her things around the room and draped her shawl over the back of a comfy looking armchair, it looked more and more like home and like she wasn't going to be leaving. Ryan reached over and squeezed my hand. He always could read my mind.

"We're missing something." Grandma looked around.

"Are you looking for this?" Ryan pulled her cookie jar out of the bag he had brought and then handed her several bags of Double Stuf Oreos.

Grandma clapped her hands.

"I'll be the most popular person here." She winked. "Maybe now they'll forgive me for beating them at poker."

Ryan laughed as Grandma launched into a rundown of all the activities she was involved in and the people she had met. She seemed really happy here. And she was her old self again.

Almost.

"When are you two going to go on a date?" Grandma asked.

Ryan opened and closed his mouth and then looked at me for help.

"Grandma," I said gently, "Ryan and I are just friends."

"I know that. But you'd make such a sweet couple."

"Ryan's gay, Grandma. Remember?"

She looked at Ryan.

"I have a boyfriend now. His name is Thomas."

"Thomas?"

"Yes. You'd really like him."

"Okay," she said. "Do you want to play cards?"

"I do," he said.

"Lucky?" Grandma asked.

"Deal me in," I told her.

I may have been desperate to go home, but at moments like this, I started to realize that Grandma was probably safer here. The disease that had made her set the house on fire wasn't something that could be cured. And in this place that now looked like home, she was surrounded by people who could help her in ways that I couldn't.

CHAPTER FIFTY-THREE
Bonding

Unlike Grandma, I added nothing to my room at Paula and Greg's house to make it any homier. Because it was never going to be home. They'd move me to the next spot eventually. I'd move into another nondescript house on a random street to sleep in a beige bedroom with an empty dresser and an old bed that had been slept in by countless others.

I went to school with a smile pasted on my face.

I worried about Grandma.

I hung out with Ryan and Thomas.

I did my chores and my homework.

I let Lucy sleep in my room.

But I didn't join any clubs.

I didn't try out for the play.

I didn't get to know Paula or Greg beyond what we talked about at meals.

I didn't make friends with the kids next door.

Because any second, that doorbell could ring and Cynthia from Children's Aid could be standing there, waiting to take me to the next place.

But there was one commitment I kept and that was to Lucy. Every night after dinner, we worked on her mother's birthday gift—a frame for Lucy's school photo. We had a cheap frame that we had glued plastic gems to in a rainbow pattern. We had finally finished it tonight, and it was sitting downstairs, packaged and ready to be dropped in the mailbox in the morning.

There was a knock on my bedroom door.

"Come in."

Lucy poked her head in.

"Sleepover?" she chirped.

"Sure," I told her. She ran in, clutching her pillow and her stuffed dog, Walter, against her chest. She dove onto the bed and slithered under the blanket.

"Tuck!" she demanded.

I got off my twin bed and walked to the other one. I tucked the blanket around her so she became a little baby burrito with only her head visible.

"Is Walter comfy?" I asked.

"Yes." She giggled. "He likes being a burrito."

"Okay then. Sleep tight, little burrito."

"Sleep tight," she said, yawning and closing her eyes.

I turned the lamp off and got into the other bed.

"Lucky?"

"Yeah?"

"I love you," Lucy called out sleepily.

I rolled over.

"I love you too, Lucy."

CHAPTER FIFTY-FOUR

Unlucky

I spent the days that followed going back and forth to school. Visiting Grandma. Hanging out with Lucy. And although I didn't change the room at Paula and Greg's house, I got comfortable. So comfortable that the last thing I expected was to find Cynthia from Children's Aid sitting at the kitchen table with Paula and Greg when Ryan and I walked in after school.

"Hi, Lucky," she said, as if seeing her didn't make my heart pound.

"Umm. Hi?"

"I'm Ryan," he held out his hand.

"Hi, Ryan. Maybe Lucky and I can speak alone for a minute?"

"Oh, sure. I can wait upstairs." He glanced at me.

"No! He can stay. If you're sending me away, he may as well hear it too."

"Lucky, we're not sending you away," Paula said, glancing at her husband. "Not exactly."

"Then what exactly is it?"

"I'm being transferred," Greg said.

"Okay."

"To Winnipeg."

"Winnipeg?"

"Yes."

"When?" I asked Cynthia.

"Six weeks," she said.

"We've been trying to find a way to take you and Lucy with us...but..." Paula shook her head.

"My grandmother is here. I wouldn't go to Winnipeg anyway," I told her coldly. Ryan rubbed my back. Usually that relaxed me, but right now it just pissed me off more.

"You can stay here with us...at least until we have to pack," Paula said.

"Just start looking for another place," I told Cynthia. "I'm ready to go as soon as you have a spot for me." I turned and walked out. Ryan trailed after me.

"Lucky," he started.

"No. Don't say anything. I don't care anyway. It's not like they were family or anything."

I turned up the hall and saw Lucy standing in her doorway. *Shit.* She had to have heard. Her face was streaked with tears as she stepped back into her room and slammed the door.

"Lucy!" I banged on her door. "I'm sorry. I didn't mean you."

"Go away!" she yelled from inside the room.

"I'm coming in," I told her, opening the door. She was sitting on her bed, her knees pulled up to her chest, and she was holding Walter tightly in her arms. "I'm sorry," I told her, sitting down on the bed beside her. "I just meant…I'm so tired of moving from place to place. I miss having a home," I admitted.

"Me too."

"Your mom will be out in a couple of weeks though," I reminded her. "You'll be back home before you know it."

"Yeah. But what about you? Where will you go?"

I shook my head.

"I don't know."

"I wish you could come and live with me."

"Me too," I told her. Lucy had become like a little sister to me.

"I don't want you to leave, Lucky," she said, her face crumbling.

"I know. Me neither. But I can call you. And visit. And send you letters and stuff."

She hugged me, and I hoped with everything I had that when she did go home to her mom, it would be the happy home she deserved.

CHAPTER FIFTY-FIVE
Leaving

Leaving Lucy was hard. Leaving Ryan again was even harder.

"I just got back," I told him, wrapping him in a hug that was going to have to last a while. My new "home" was on the other end of the city. Nowhere near my school. Or Ryan. Or Lucy. Or even Grandma.

"You're not moving to another country, Lucky," he said, squeezing the breath out of me.

"I know. But I got used to seeing you every day again. It's gonna suck not having you around." We were sitting on the front steps of Paula and Greg's house, waiting for Cynthia to pick me up and take me away to Home #4, as we were calling it, completely ironically of course.

"I'll come see you. And you can take the bus to visit me. Maybe they'll let you spend the night sometimes." He was sniffling and trying not to cry. I wiped my nose on the sleeve of my hoodie. "That's so gross, Lucky," he said, laughing.

"Shut up," I told him, hugging him tightly again. It might be the last chance I had for a while.

Cynthia pulled into the driveway then.

"I have to go," I told him as Lucy flew out of the house to say good-bye. She'd be staying a little longer so her mother could find a job and a place to stay. "I'll text you when I get there."

He nodded.

"And I'll see you soon," he promised.

I hugged Lucy.

"You help your mom when you get a new home with her, okay? And I'll come and see you when I can."

"Okay." She smiled.

"And you have my phone number, right?"

"Yes. I'll miss you, Lucky."

"You too." I let go of her and walked down the stairs, then turned to the couple standing in the doorway. "Thanks for everything," I said to Paula and Greg. They smiled.

"Good luck," Greg said.

I climbed into the Prius and waved as Cynthia pulled out of another driveway and headed down another street to another neighborhood and another foster home.

CHAPTER FIFTY-SIX
Home #4

The doorbell at House #4 played the theme song to *Doctor Who*. I almost cracked a smile when I heard it.

Almost.

A woman with a wide, welcoming smile opened the door.

"Hi, Lucky! I'm Janine." She extended a hand to me. "We're happy to have you here. Welcome to our home."

Another "home" on another nondescript street whose name I won't bother remembering.

"This is Mia," Janine tells me, gesturing to a girl the same age as me. "And this is Isabelle," she says, nodding at another girl who is a little older, I think. "Mia, why don't you show Lucky her room."

I nod. I don't smile. I just follow Mia up the stairs to a room with empty dove-gray walls and that looks just like the last three rooms, with a window overlooking a street that could be anywhere and would never really feel like home. I didn't even bother to unpack. Just tossed my stuff into the corner.

"This was my room when I first came," Mia was babbling at me, "but I moved into a better room when the last girl left." I had a feeling Mia was one of those girls who always had to be better than everyone else. I'd have to keep an eye on her.

"Cool," I told her, not really wanting to engage in conversation.

"Yeah. Isabelle has the biggest room because she's the oldest, but when she ages out, I'm taking her room."

Wow.

"Janine's a teacher at my school. Well...I guess your school too now."

"Yeah."

"So what do you do for fun?" Mia asked, apparently trying to decide if I was cool enough for her. Something told me I wouldn't be.

"I don't know," I told her.

"Do you go to the mall? Watch *The Kardashians* or *Teen Mom?* Get your nails done?"

"Ummm. Not really. I read comics," I admitted.

"Oh *gawd!* Another dork in the house." She flounced out of the room and left me alone—finally. I lay down on the bed that was not too soft and not too hard. Every foster family seemed to shop in the same place, I thought. I was just drifting off when there was a knock at the door.

"I really don't want to watch *The Kardashians* with you," I called out.

"Well good," a voice laughed from the doorway. "I can't stand those people. I don't know how Mia can watch that show."

"Oh, sorry." I sat up as my new foster mother stepped into the room.

"It's okay, Lucky," she said, smiling. "Are you settled in?"

I glanced over at my backpack that was still full of all my stuff and shrugged.

"I guess."

"Good. Well, I just wanted to say good night and let you know that if there's anything you need, I'm right down the hall."

"Thanks, but I'm good."

"Okay. Is there anything you'd like to get for your room? Do you want to paint the walls or anything?"

"Why?" I asked. I mean…it was a foster home. It wasn't like I'd be there long enough to even settle in, if my past experiences were any indication.

"To make it feel more like you," she said. "More like home."

"I haven't spent more than a couple of weeks in one place since my grandmother burned our house down. I doubt I'll be here any longer." I was being bitchy. I knew it. But I couldn't help myself. There wasn't much point in making friends with these people. I'd made that mistake before, I thought bitterly, remembering Charlie, Jake, and Lucy.

Janine smiled kindly despite my rudeness.

"All right. Just let me know if you change your mind," she said. "Sleep well, Lucky."

"Thanks."

It wasn't that I didn't appreciate the offer. But honestly… what was the point?

CHAPTER FIFTY-SEVEN

Janine

When I opened my eyes the next morning, I couldn't remember for a second where I was. It was pretty disorienting when every room you stayed in looked the same as any other.

I showered quickly and pulled one of the sweaters Grandma had made me out of my backpack. It was a soft gray, and when I wore it, I felt like she was there with me somehow. It was getting small though, tight where it had been loose only a few months ago. I pulled at it and then decided it was okay to wear a few more times.

"Holy shit! What are you wearing? God, Lucky. If that sweater was any tighter, it would pop right off. Or is that the point?" Mia asked.

"My grandmother made it for me," I said, coloring and pulling at it, willing it to stretch a bit.

"Well the boys are going to loooooove it," she said. She

turned when Isabelle walked in. "Hey Izzy. Check out the slutty sweater on Lucky." She laughed.

"Leave her alone," Isabelle told her. "And don't call me Izzy. Do I look like a frickin' Izzy to you?" she grumbled.

"Language." Janine walked into the kitchen, catching the last bit of the conversation.

"Sorry, Janine," Isabelle said.

"Did you sleep well, Lucky?" Janine asked.

"I guess so," I told her.

"That's good. All right girls. We better get moving." She grabbed her keys while I looked at her blankly. "I work at your school," she said. "So I drive everyone."

"Oh! Right." I grabbed my bag and followed everyone out the door.

"Mia, can you take Lucky to the office to get her schedule?" Janine asked the second we pulled into the parking lot.

"I guess. But I can't stay. I have to get to class early today."

"It's fine. I can find it," I told them both.

"No. I can show you the office." Mia grabbed my arm and pulled me along behind her. I yanked my arm out of her grasp.

"What's your problem?" she asked.

"Nothing. I just don't appreciate being manhandled."

She smirked.

"Dressed like that?" she asked.

"Jesus, Mia. You're a girl. Do you really think it's helpful to slut shame other girls?" I asked her.

Mia shrugged. "Whatever. Here's the office." She turned, elbowing me firmly in the ribs.

"What the *hell*, Mia?" I pushed her. Hard. She hit the wall and bounced back, her eyes bright. Like she was excited at the prospect of a fight.

"You want to go? I'm ready anytime you are. You think I'm afraid of you?" Mia yelled in my face. I felt my fists clenching. I pulled my arm back, ready to hit her so hard, it would wipe the smirk off her face permanently.

"Lucky!" Janine was behind us suddenly. She pulled me away from Mia before I could launch an attack. "What are you doing?"

"I didn't start it! She did! She elbowed me."

Janine looked toward Mia.

"Mia, get to class."

"Janine, she's a liar!"

"Now."

Janine left no room to argue. She held Mia's gaze until the girl grabbed her bag off the floor and huffed away. We were there early so the halls were still empty, thankfully. No one except Janine had witnessed our almost-fight.

"Let's go to my class and talk," Janine said. I followed her down the hall, my heart beating hard. She led me into an empty class and gestured toward the rows of desks. "Sit."

I didn't. I couldn't calm down enough to sit so I paced in front of her desk. Mia had been all over me since I got up this morning. If Janine hadn't intervened, I would have been in another fight and probably sent to another school. From the look on Janine's face, she had Cynthia on speed dial and was about to push SEND.

"Just get it over with." I spat the words out at her.

"Get what over with?" she asked, looking like she legitimately didn't know what I meant.

"I know Cynthia had to have told you what happened to me. The fights I got into. How I put my foster brother in the hospital."

"She told me it was a terrible accident and he's fine," she said mildly.

"So? When does that matter to anyone? When does anyone care *why* I do anything? Why I threatened the foster father who got into my bed? Why I was fighting Elyse? Who cares what made me do those things? I know you don't. You're going to call Cynthia, and I'll get sent to another foster home with another foster parent who doesn't give a damn about me. Go ahead. You're going to send me away so just go on and do it."

"Sit down, Lucky." This time, I sat, my chest heaving. "I saw your file. I know what happened to you at your first foster home. I know what was done to you and that you defended yourself. Good for you. I don't blame you one bit." I looked at her, surprised. "And I know you fought with a racist girl who spat at you and called you and your foster brother names. I don't even blame you for that, really. You've been through a lot. I don't condone fighting. But sometimes we have to fight to survive. And you've had to survive since you went into foster care. Maybe before. And maybe you'll tell me about it someday. I was in foster care too, you know."

"You were?"

She nodded. "I was. And I fought. And I had some pretty shitty foster parents. So I get it. But you don't have to fight here. Mia will push your buttons, but she's not a bad person. She has her own story, just like you. I'm not going to call Cynthia because you almost got into a fight, Lucky. If I called her every time Mia almost got into a fight, she'd be here every other day," she said, laughing. "But you need to try to stay out of trouble. If you have a problem, come to me and we'll figure it out. Okay?"

I shrugged.

"I know you don't trust me yet. I get that too. But I'll earn your trust. I promise you that. Do you remember where the office is?" she asked.

"Yeah."

"Then go get your timetable and get to class."

I left her there. I didn't trust her, but the fact that she had been a foster kid herself made me a little more comfortable with her.

It took about thirty seconds to get my timetable and directions to my first class. Which led to the second class. It was a rat race. Just like any other high school. Get from one class to another and fly under the radar.

I was back to not knowing anyone, and I wasn't about to spend my lunch with Mia and I didn't see Isabelle. I wandered around instead, getting acclimated and nibbling the bagel Janine had packed for me. At the end of one of the labyrinthine hallways, I found the library. Curious if it was going to be worth visiting, I pushed the door open and fell down a rabbit hole of familiarity. The hush of people working at tables. The click of computer keys. The smell of books. I closed my eyes and inhaled deeply.

"Are you going to stand there blocking the door all day?" someone behind me asked. I turned and saw Isabelle.

"Oh, sorry!"

She nodded and went around me, dropping a pile of graphic novels on the return cart. *Graphic novels?* I rushed over and caught her as she dropped her backpack on a table and pulled out a binder.

"Where did you find those?" I asked, pointing at the graphic novels she had put down. She had discarded *The Sandman: Overture*, which was my absolute favorite.

"Last aisle," she said, nodding in the direction she was referring to, before putting her headphones on and drowning me out. I heard the tinny bassline of whatever she was listening to and stepped away, mouthing my thanks.

I already had *The Sandman: Overture* back in my room, so I headed off to the last aisle.

Holy crap.

I was standing in a long aisle of comic books and graphic novels. And they weren't all ancient! I saw *X-Men* and *Batman.* I saw *Spider-Man* and *Doctor Strange*. I was in heaven. I pulled a bunch off the shelves and sank down the floor. I knew where I'd be spending my lunch break from now on.

I barely noticed when someone else came down the aisle, I was so into the world of Marvel that I didn't even look up. Until she cleared her throat.

"Hey. You don't have *Astro City* in that pile, do you?" Isabelle asked.

"Oh. Hey. Ummm...yeah." I went through the pile until I found it and held it out to her.

"Are you sure?" she asked.

"Yeah. I've read it before," I told her.

"Me too." The corners of her mouth lifted a bit as she took it from me and walked away.

If I had to live with someone like Mia, at least there was another comic nerd in the house to even things out. Even if she didn't talk much.

CHAPTER FIFTY-EIGHT

Days Go By

RYAN:	So how's the new place?
ME:	Ok I guess. Not home. Janine is nice. And the older kid is ok. Quiet. Likes comics. But the other one is a jerk. Kim Kardashian is her role model
RYAN:	Brutal. Just ignore her
ME:	I try
RYAN:	Wanna meet after school? I can pick you up
ME:	Coffee?
RYAN:	Sure

Ryan was waiting outside the school for me. He leaped out of his car and gave me a huge hug and a kiss on the cheek.

"You must have missed me." I grinned.

"You know I did. School sucks without you."

"Even with Thomas?" I asked.

"Well...he makes it bearable. So where do we go for coffee around here?" he asked, turning around and speeding away from the school.

Because we were in the city and there's literally a Starbucks on every corner, we ended up at one with a latte each.

"I have to be back for dinner," I warned him, blowing on my coffee before taking a tentative sip.

"Okay." He settled into his chair. "So how's the guy situation?" he asked.

"Nonexistent. Honestly, I'll never meet a guy if I don't stay in one place more than a few weeks at a time. I haven't even thought about dating, to be honest."

Ryan studied me for a long minute, then smiled.

"Really? Not even that guy Jake?" he asked.

"No! Well...maybe," I admitted. "But I'll probably never see him again, so what's the point?"

Ryan gawked at me.

"He lives in the suburbs, Lucky. Not another country."

"Yeah well..." I trailed off, sipping my drink. "Anyway, I can't think about guys right now. Not with my grandma...the way she is. I'll just live vicariously through you and Thomas."

Ryan smiled happily and filled me in on everything Thomas-related for an hour before driving me "home."

CHAPTER FIFTY-NINE
Mia and Isabelle

I walked into the house smiling and feeling almost like my old self after hanging out with Ryan, but Mia pounced the second I came in.

"Your boyfriend is cute," she said. "Why didn't you invite him in for dinner?"

"He's not my boyfriend," I told her. I immediately regretted it. It was none of her business, and I suddenly knew there was nothing I could say that was going to make her shut up and leave me alone.

"Oh really? Because I saw the way you were draped all over him, Lucky."

"Are you serious?" I was trying so hard to get along here, and she was making it impossible. "I hugged him good-bye. We've been friends since we were seven," I told her.

"Awww. And now you're sleeping with him?" she prodded.

"Oh my god, Mia. Ryan's gay. Not that it's any of your business."

"You've got a gay boyfriend?" she crowed. "Aren't you afraid you're going to catch something?"

"Am I afraid of catching 'the gay' from him?" I asked sarcastically. "Not really. Also, you're an idiot."

"Janine's gay," she whispered.

"So what?"

"So aren't you worried she's going to hit on you?" Mia asked.

"You're such a homophobe, Mia," I told her. Honestly, people could be so stupid.

"She really is." Isabelle wandered into the kitchen then, overhearing the very end of the conversation.

"Whatever," Mia said, turning and leaving me alone, finally, with Isabelle. My phone chose that moment to ring.

"Hello? Hi Grandma. What's wrong? No. I can't come tonight." I glanced over at Isabelle but she had her headphones on again. "What do you need me to get? Well, can't it wait until tomorrow? I understand you have a cold, but isn't there a nurse or someone who can bring you medicine? Do you really need that particular tea? Okay. Hang on a second." I rifled through the cupboards and miraculously found ginger lemon tea. "All right, we have some. I have to be here for dinner, but I'll come tonight. Do you at least have honey? Okay. Love you too."

Isabelle was watching me stuff a couple of the teabags into the pocket of my hoodie.

"It's for my grandma," I told her. Isabelle raised an eyebrow at me. “She has a cold. And Alzheimer’s. Not that you asked or anything,” I mumbled.

“I’m sorry,” she said softly before disappearing out of the room.

“Thanks,” I called after her.

I had the tea. Now all I had to do was get it to my Grandma before she went to bed, without getting caught.

CHAPTER SIXTY
An Adventure

I had to be careful trying to get out of the house. I didn't want Mia or Isabelle to catch me. And I sure as hell needed to avoid Janine. I faked a headache and retired to my room, telling Janine I was going to bed early, and then snuck back down when I heard her turn the TV on. She liked to watch her British crime shows while we were doing homework or were otherwise engaged. If I could get past the living room, it would be a straight shot to the front door.

I made sure I had the tea bags for Grandma, and I grabbed my wallet out of my backpack. But I had forgotten that I paid for coffee with Ryan. I was flat broke. And my transit card had expired. Which was a big issue when I needed a way to get to and from the care facility. I crept downstairs, trying to figure out what I was going to do and saw Janine's purse sitting on the counter where she had left it. I stared at it. There's no way

Janine would miss five dollars, right? I argued with myself. It was stealing. But I'd pay her back somehow. Maybe Grandma could give me some money. I edged toward the bag and then snagged her wallet out. I grabbed a five-dollar bill and put the wallet back, feeling guilty as hell.

Stuffing the money in my pocket, I edged past the living room and out the front door.

I felt guilty all the way to the bus stop.

I felt guilty on the bus. And on the subway.

And I felt guilty riding yet another bus to the home.

By the time I walked into the building to see Grandma, the guilt was eating away at me. I stuffed it down as far as I could and walked up to the front desk.

"Hi, I'm here to see my grandmother. Daisy Robinson."

"It's past visiting hours," the receptionist told me, frowning.

"I...didn't realize there were specific hours. Umm...look. She's sick with a cold, and I came all the way from the suburbs to bring her the tea she likes. Can I just drop it off and make sure she's okay?"

"Well...I guess as long as you don't stay."

"I won't. I promise."

"You know where to go?"

"Yes Ma'am. Thank you."

I took off down the hall before she could change her mind. It was much quieter at night. The halls were mostly empty, with only a few people walking around or chatting.

I knocked quietly on Grandma's door.

"Yes?"

She sounded congested, poor thing. I poked my head in.

"Hi, Grandma. I brought you your tea."

"Tea?"

"Yes. Your lemon ginger…or ginger lemon…whatever it is. I brought it for you." I held out the tea bags proudly.

"What are you talking about?" she asked, looking confused and, if I'm being honest, kind of pissed off.

"You called me and told me you were sick and needed tea." What the hell was going on?

"Your father made me tea!" she told me. She was getting angry now.

I sat down heavily on the bed, fighting back tears. She wasn't getting better.

"Christina?"

"It's Lucky, Grandma."

"Lucky?"

"That's right."

"What are you doing here?"

"I brought you tea, Grandma."

"Oh, that was so sweet of you!" she exclaimed. She had no memory of calling me. And I had stolen money to come.

"I can't stay, Grandma. But would you like me to make you tea?"

"No thank you, sweetheart. Your grandfather made me some earlier."

I didn't have the heart to argue. Or explain. Or correct her.

"Okay. I should go then. Here's the tea bags if you want

more. I love you, Grandma. I hope you feel better soon," I told her, kissing her on the cheek.

"Thank you," she said, smiling happily and oblivious to all she was losing day by day.

CHAPTER SIXTY-ONE
Getting Caught

There was a jumper on the subway, according to the other passengers, so I sat on the train for twice as long, knowing that there was no way I was going to be able to sneak back in. Especially if Janine had gone to bed.

I didn't even have a key.

By the time I got back to the foster home, it was going on ten o'clock. The lights were on downstairs, but I thought I could still at least try to get in without being noticed.

No such luck.

Janine was sitting facing the door when I walked in. She stared at me, her face unreadable. I waited for her to start yelling. To tell me that she had called Cynthia, and I should go get my things. I waited for her to say *something*. Then, before I could say a word myself, she jumped up and grabbed me in a hug that knocked the breath out of me.

"Lucky, where the hell have you been? I was worried sick! I called and called you!"

I realized on the bus into the city that I had forgotten my phone that was plugged in upstairs.

"Umm..." A hug was the last thing I had been expecting. "I'm sorry, Janine. I forgot my phone. My grandmother is sick and she needed me to bring her some tea they didn't have at the place she's living."

Janine was still hugging me.

"I thought I could be back before you knew I was gone," I admitted. She let me go then and held me at arm's length, studying my face.

"Lucky, you can't just leave without telling me. If Mia hadn't noticed you were gone..." she trailed off. Mia! Of course she had told on me, the little rat.

"I'm sorry. I just...she said she needed it...." It sounded lame. Even to me. "And Janine? I'm really sorry, but I borrowed...I *took*...five dollars for the bus and train. I'll pay you back. I promise."

She shook her head.

"I can't have you running around the city, spending hours on the bus or subway..."

"I know. I'm sorry."

"So the next time you want to go see your grandmother, or if she needs anything, you tell me and I'll drive you."

"Wait...what?"

"And you can do the dishes for the rest of the week *and* the laundry to pay back the bus fare. Okay?"

"I...okay. Of course. Thank you." I was staring at her. It's not like no one else had been nice to me since I left home. But no one except Janine really seemed to understand what I was going through with my grandma. And they certainly never offered to drive me to see her. Except Ryan, and he was family.

"You're welcome. And you don't need to steal, Lucky. If you need something, just ask. Now go upstairs and get to bed," she told me. "You must be exhausted." She smiled and rubbed my arm.

I walked upstairs feeling kind of numb. I had expected the absolute worst from Janine. But she wasn't mad. And she understood how important it was for me to be there for my grandmother. I opened the door to my room and stepped inside. There was a reading lamp on the night table that had been bare when I left the house earlier. There was also a book. I stepped over to see what it was. There was a note on top:

I thought you might like this. I used to sneak these into my room when I was your age.

—Janine

It was a copy of *The Shining* by Stephen King.

CHAPTER SIXTY-TWO

Getting Along

Mia and Janine were making pancakes when I came downstairs the next day. Mia was telling Janine about some Kardashian or another—seriously, what was her obsession with the stupid Kardashians?—and Isabelle was reading at the table.

"Thought you could use a sleep in," Janine called out. "Are you hungry?"

"Yes, please." I accepted a steaming plate of pancakes and nodded my thanks at Isabelle when she slid the syrup toward me. "Thanks for the book! I started it last night. My grandma loves Stephen King."

She smiled at me and showed Mia how to flip the pancakes into the air without letting them fall on the floor. Mia tried and promptly lost one. I rolled my eyes but Janine patted her on the back.

"Don't worry. We've got lots of batter and the floor needed to be washed today anyway."

The pancakes were delicious, and the sweet, earthy taste of maple syrup reminded me of being at home with my grandparents.

"What are you smiling about, Lucky?" Janine called out, scraping a bit of batter off the floor where Mia had dripped it.

"Maple butter."

"What's maple butter?" Isabelle asked, peeking over the top of her book.

"It's amazing. It's like a thicker version of...well, maple syrup and butter."

"For waffles?" Mia asked, interested despite herself.

"No. Well, I guess. But we used to make bannock and put it on that." My mouth watered just thinking about it.

"What's bannock?" Mia asked.

"It's a kind of bread...we're Cree. My grandparents and I. We'd make that and put maple butter or strawberry jam on it. My grandpa and I could eat a whole batch of bannock in one day." I laughed.

"Maybe you could teach us," Janine said. "Mia loves to cook, don't you, Mia?" Mia shrugged.

"I'm not sure I'd like Indian food," she sniffed.

So, homophobic *and* racist.

"I'd try it," Isabelle said. I smiled at her.

"I'll make some later, if you want," I told Janine and Isabelle, ignoring Mia. "After I do the dishes, of course."

"Of course." Janine smiled. "Do I need to pick anything up?"

"Nah. You've probably got everything I need."

I stood up and took my plate to the sink.

CHAPTER SIXTY-THREE
Belonging

The more I decided to try to get along with everyone and not be so...testy, the more Janine tried to make my room feel like a place where I belonged. After the lamp and the book, she hung a poster of Alan Rickman reading a book on one wall and David Tennant standing in front of the TARDIS on another. How she knew I was both a *Harry Potter* and *Doctor Who* fan, I had no idea. But now, instead of staring at the ceiling at night, I could look at the Doctor and remember watching episodes with Grandpa, while Grandma sat with us, reading a book. She never did understand our *Doctor Who* obsession.

Janine knocked on my door.

"I found this for you at a garage sale," she said, pulling a bookcase into the room. "Where do you want it?"

"Uh, over there, I guess." I pointed at the wall under the Alan Rickman poster.

"Yes! Perfect." She put it down and stood back, then adjusted it to the right a little. "Now you just need a good reading chair," she said.

"You don't have to buy me things," I told her. She looked at me kindly.

"It's my job to make this a home for you, Lucky. And that means giving you a room that's yours. A place you can go to get away from everyone and feel comfortable."

"Why? I'm going to go back home when my grandmother is better," I said, wishing it were true and terrified that it wasn't. "Or I'll be sent to another home as soon as I start getting comfortable here."

"I don't want you to go to another home, Lucky. You're welcome here as long as you need a place to stay. I promise you that."

"You say that now," I told her. "But as soon as I get into trouble, you'll have Cynthia and her Prius here before I have time to pack my stuff."

"You've had some pretty crappy homes, haven't you?" Janine asked, tilting her head.

"You could say that," I admitted. "Some of them were nice, but they sent me away anyway."

"I won't send you away, Lucky," Janine said gently. "You can trust me."

I nodded at her. "Thanks," I said, meaning it but not daring to really believe her.

"I thought you might like to visit your grandma today," Janine said.

"Really?"

"Yeah. I have to go into the city to pick something up anyway."

"Okay. Thanks!"

"Get ready, and we can go as soon as you'd like."

I nodded my thanks and wondered if Janine would lend me the money to buy Grandma some Oreos.

Double Stuf or it doesn't count.

CHAPTER SIXTY-FOUR

For Sale

Grandma emptied the bag of Oreos I had brought her into her cookie jar. I had been ready for the worst, but she was back to her old self today.

"Everyone has been coming by and depleting my supplies," she told me. "It's made me pretty popular around here. Especially with the residents who are on a low sugar diet."

"Grandma! You're not giving cookies to diabetics or anything, are you?"

"I don't know everyone's medical history! But come to think of it, I should probably be asking them before I let them eat my Oreos. And maybe regular stuf instead of double from now on."

I laughed.

"Okay, Grandma."

She picked up a deck of cards and shuffled them. She had promised to teach me to play poker.

"I need to talk to you about something," she said. "You better sit down."

"Okay. What is it?"

She took my hands.

"You know I love you—"

"Grandma, you're scaring me."

"I'm sorry. I'm scared too, sometimes," she admitted. "I'm scared because I know that my good days are going to get fewer and farther between. There may very well come a time when I won't recognize you." Her eyes welled up, but she swallowed hard and kept going. "I'm not ever going to be able to go home, Lucky. And I'm so sorry for that. Because it means you can't go home either. Maybe someday your mother will clean herself up and be the mother you deserve. But for now, you're in a safe place. And it'll have to be home."

I was gripping her hands in mine and willing all of this to be a dream. But she was right. I knew she was right. And I owed it to her to listen.

"I still have more good days than bad." She smiled. "So I have to make decisions for myself and for you before that changes. The director here helped me find a good lawyer to help outline the kind of care I want. I don't want you to have to make those decisions, Lucky. She also helped me put the house on the market."

"What?" I gasped. "No!"

"Yes." She touched my face gently. "It's time, Lucky."

"But it's our home," I told her, forcing back tears.

"It was. And we had a wonderful life there with your grandfather. But it's time to let someone else make a life there."

"Okay." I nodded. She was right. We weren't ever going home again.

"I'm putting the money from the house into an account for you so you can go to university. And I'm updating my will to make sure your mother can't touch it." She smiled sadly.

I opened my mouth but then just nodded as she kissed my cheek.

"It's what your grandfather would want. And it's what I want."

"Can I go back and get anything else we need before they sell it?" I asked.

She smiled. "Of course, you can. And bring me the photo albums out of the closet, if you would. They're on the top shelf."

I promised I would, and then I let her deal the cards, trying to focus on learning the intricacies of poker and not on the fact that someone else would be living in our house.

Janine knocked on the door an hour later.

"Hi, Mrs. Robinson," she said, smiling and holding out her hand. "I'm Janine. Lucky's foster mom." Grandma stood and pulled her into a hug.

"Thank you for taking care of my Lucky girl," Grandma told her.

"It's my pleasure. Lucky is an amazing girl."

"Yes, she is."

They made small talk while I gathered my things and then kissed Grandma good-bye.

"I'll see you soon, Grandma," I told her.

We walked into the hall and I followed Janine, zombie-like, to the parking lot. I got into the car automatically, put on my seat belt, and waited for Janine to get in and take me back. She got in, then turned to me with an odd look on her face.

"Lucky, are you okay?" she asked.

And that was all it took. I burst into tears. Noisy sobs that came from so deep inside that my whole body was shaking.

God, I hated to cry.

Janine unhooked my seat belt and pulled me into a hug, rubbing my back while I wet the shoulder of her sweater with tears and snot. She didn't tell me that everything was going to be okay. She didn't try to do that thing adults do where they try to fix all your problems. Janine just let me cry and held me until I was ready to go home.

CHAPTER SIXTY-FIVE

A New Life

Mia pushed past me in the kitchen, nearly making me drop my cereal bowl.

"Watch it," I told her.

"God, Lucky...don't you have any clothes that fit? Or do you just like showing off your tits?" she asked, sneering at my sweater. I didn't really feel like explaining to her that my grandmother made it for me and it was one of the few things I had from home. At least until Ryan could find the time to take me this week to pick up more stuff. I thought briefly about hitting her, but that wasn't really me either. I chose to ignore her instead.

"Are all Indians deaf or just you? Or maybe you're stupid? Is that it?" she taunted.

I clenched my fists but didn't make a move toward her.

"Go ahead," she said. "Give it your best shot. I've fought girls more savage than you, Pocahontas."

I took a step toward her just as Isabelle walked in.

"Go get ready for school, Mia," she told her. Mia looked at her, then at me, then shrugged.

"She's not worth it anyway." She walked out, hitting me hard with her shoulder as she passed.

"I could have taken her," I told Isabelle.

"Probably. But she doesn't fight so she can win."

"Then why fight?" I asked.

"I don't know. I think it's so she can feel something."

"What do you mean?"

Isabelle took a banana and sat down, peeling it thoughtfully and methodically before she answered.

"Mia and her family were in a car accident. Mia was the only survivor. She doesn't talk about it, but she feels guilty."

"For what?"

"For being the one to live."

I thought about that. I could almost understand. And if I'm being honest, as horrible as she was, I felt bad for her. I went up to my room and sat on my bed, looking around at the things Janine kept bringing in and leaving. A box of books she said she had bought at the secondhand bookstore but that somehow included the brand-new Adam Silvera book. And the piles of comics she somehow "found." I had even found a pile of new clothes in one of my dresser drawers alongside the few things I had finally broken down and unpacked. Slowly, this place was becoming home. And like it or not, that made Mia family.

I looked through the pile of comics that were my absolute favorites and pulled out my pride and joy—the brand-new *Captain Marvel.* She kind of looked a little like Mia. I walked down the hall to Mia's room and slid it under her door. I listened and heard her walk over and pick it up. She'd either fling open the door and throw it in my face or check it out. I waited and didn't get hit by a flying comic, so I assumed she was going to read it.

Hey, it was a start.

CHAPTER SIXTY-SIX

Happy Birthday

Grandma was sitting behind me in my room, brushing my hair. I always loved when she brushed it. Janine had gotten her a day pass and driven her all the way here so she could help me celebrate my birthday. As she helped me get ready, Ryan and Thomas and Lucy were all downstairs, helping Janine and Isabelle get lunch ready.

"I like your room," Grandma said. "It's really…you." I grinned as she pinned part of my hair back.

"I know. Janine is always finding cool stuff. Like that rug. And I brought your throw pillow for my bed. It made a big difference bringing some stuff from home," I told her. She nodded. She had felt the same way when Ryan and I had brought some more things from the house for her room.

"You have a wonderful home here, Lucky."

"I know." I did too. Even Mia had lightened up on me lately. She had left *Captain Marvel* outside my door, so I chose another comic I thought she'd like and slid it under her door. She hadn't said anything to me but she did keep reading them. I was shocked that the Kardashian-loving Mia really loved to read.

The doorbell rang just as Grandma and I came down.

"Lucky, could you get that?" Janine called out.

"Sure." I opened the door, calling over my shoulder for my grandmother to head to the kitchen. I stopped mid-sentence, then screamed.

"OHMYGOD!"

I threw myself at Jake and Charlie, who were standing on the front porch, clutching gift bags and grinning widely. We were quickly tangled in a three-way hug when Ryan cleared his throat behind me.

"Well? Aren't you going to invite them in?" he asked, smiling happily.

"You did this?" I asked Ryan, feeling a familiar little flutter when Jake smiled at me.

"Of course."

I untangled myself and led the boys in.

"Thank you," I whispered to Ryan, planting a quick kiss on his cheek before heading through the living room where Mia was hanging streamers.

"She's coming!" Mia yelled out. There was a commotion in the kitchen. I led Grandma in and was greeted by every single thing Janine had ever made that I loved. Fried chicken

When the table was cleared, Janine brought out a chocolate cake, candles blazing, as everyone sang "Happy Birthday."

"Make a wish!" Lucy screamed, laughing maniacally.

I stared at the candles, watching the wax drip onto the icing.

"Any minute now, Lucky. Preferably before we have to call the fire department." Ryan laughed.

What did you wish for when life didn't turn out the way you planned? When the place you ended up finally felt like home and the people around you made up one incredibly weird but amazing family?

I closed my eyes and took a breath and finally, I blew out the candles.

Acknowledgments

So many people supported me in the writing of this book and I hope you know how grateful I am to all of you.

To all my writer friends who are a constant source of support and encouragement. Mel and Karen in particular—my waffle buddies. You inspire me constantly.

To my amazing friend Robin Stevenson for answering my panicked emails and pointing me in the right direction when I was trying to make sure I got this book right.

To Heather MacKenzie. A million thanks for answering my questions and making me feel much more confident that I got Lucky's story right.

To Amy Tompkins, my incredible agent. I couldn't ask for a more supportive and amazing champion. Thanks for everything you do. I truly couldn't imagine a better partnership.

And to the team at Second Story Press for letting me write another book for you and trusting me with this one in particular. You've had my back from Day One and I appreciate it more than you know. Margie, Emma, Kathryn, and Melissa. Thank you, thank you, thank you.

Lastly, thanks to my family for letting me disappear into my studio to write. You guys are the best. And Taylor, your late-night text when you finished the book was the best review I'll ever receive.

About the Author

MELANIE FLORENCE is an award-winning writer of Cree and Scottish heritage. Her picture book *Stolen Words* was the winner of the Ruth and Sylvia Schwartz Children's Book Award. Her first picture book, *Missing Nimama*, won the TD Canadian Children's Literature Award. She is the author of the YA novels *The Missing, He Who Dreams, Rez Runaway,* and *One Night*. She also wrote the nonfiction books *Righting Canada's Wrongs: Residential Schools* and *Jordin Tootoo: The Highs and Lows of the First Inuit to Play in the NHL*. Melanie lives with her husband and two children in Toronto.

Visit her website www.melanieflorence.com